# THE SEA CHILD

# THE
# SEA CHILD

## Carolyn Sloan

HOLIDAY HOUSE / NEW YORK

Copyright © Carolyn Sloan 1987
First American publication 1988 by Holiday House, Inc.
Printed in the United States of America

Library of Congress Cataloging-in-Publication Data

Sloan, Carolyn.
The sea child.

Summary: A mysterious "sea child" ventures into a
nearby village where she meets a lonely nine-year-old.
[1. Fantasy]   I. Title.
PZ7.S6325Se   1988     [Fic]     88-45273
ISBN 0-8234-0723-3

# One

A fishing boat came within a mile of The Sands one afternoon before the high spring tides. The sea tossed it about like a cork float, a teasing game, yet the sea hinted it could get rough and become an enemy.

Jessie saw it from a fold in the dunes where she was picking the new shoots of sand sedge. She dropped her basket and plunged and skidded through the soft sand leading back to the house. Bates, her seagull, watched her with comic surprise and then sailed grandly after her.

"Danny! Danny! There's a boat...a boat and *people*...it's coming here!" Danny threw the nets he was mending away from him and grabbed Jessie roughly.

"What sort of boat?"

"A lugger like yours, I think...with two sails set and..."

"They didn't see you?"

"No, but..."

"Get inside. Stay there." He dragged her into the house, to her room.

"Danny, let me look, just see what they're like."

"No. You'll stay here, Jessie or...or I'll bar the door."

"You wouldn't do that, would you, Danny?" His tense face told her that he would. She sat on the floor and stared at him. Her father had never been afraid of anything. Jessie thought he couldn't be. But he was now. He stood in the doorway listening, though there was nothing to hear. His pale eyes stared at the outer wall as if he could see through it. Jessie felt twisted up inside with unknown feelings.

"I'll stay here," she said quietly. "But they'll come anyway, won't they?" He shook his head. "They can't. No one can bring a boat in here except me now."

"They could jump out of the boat," said Jessie, catching his fear, "and swim to the shore."

Her father shook his head again, faster this time. "Impossible. No one can swim in those waters, they'd drown."

"I can."

"Yes. You can." He gave her a strangely long look and then strode away.

Bates landed clumsily on the windowsill and balanced on his strongest leg, pecking at a shipworm hole in the rotting shutter.

"Come here, Bates. Bates! Stay with me, please..." He had gone, too. Jessie lay back on the sandy floor staring bleakly at the rafters high above. The twisted-up feeling was worse now. She knew it was something to do with Danny being afraid. Something to do with the way he had looked at her because she could swim in any sea, knowing she would not drown.

But more than that, it was something to do with the boat coming and bringing people close.

Jessie had never seen another person in all her life. Only Danny.

Bates knew about other people, especially people in boats, and he flew out to this one to see what fish they had caught, and what they might throw overboard for him. But the men were not fishing, and even a seagull could tell that one of them was not a fisherman at all, but a land-man, huddled in a high collared coat, who sat uneasily in the boat and braced himself jerkily against the rhythm of the sea. He was Robbins, a reporter from a London paper. He had travelled four days from London to see The Sands, and now that he was close he was feeling seasick and angry with Riley, the boatman.

"Get closer, right in," he said, trying to train his spy glass on the land and bruising his eye socket as the boat fell into a trough in the waves.

"No, sir. This is close as I dare. Closer than most'd dare. Turning back now."

"I paid you to get right in there. We're a mile off yet."

"I'm not risking my boat nor my life," shouted Riley against the rising wind. "We'll be over the sunken village if I don't put her about."

"Good, good. Go on. Where is it?"

"On line with them rocks, a hundred yards or so in front of us."

"Can you see it? The village, man, can you see it?"

"It's dark down there now, sir. No one would try. We're going about."

"No! Keep going. There's another sovereign for you if you try."

"Keep a hundred sovereigns, I'll not do it," shouted Riley. "Weather's worsening, see how the water's boiling, like? It'll get worse. They don't want us there."

Robbins tried to get up and lurched towards him. "They? Who's *they*? You said..."

A wave came across the boat, caught Robbins and sprawled him, spluttering, onto the fishy, slippery deck. Riley started to laugh. "That one were aimed right at you!" he muttered. But there was one for him too and he ducked beneath it. The boat plunged suddenly, as if a gaping hole had opened up in the sea. Riley fought to control the boat but the sails would not obey him, the keel would not grip and the rudder hung uselessly above the waves. A viciously veering wind blew gustily; the sea seemed almost hostile. Robbins clutched the mast, swearing. Riley prayed a sailor's prayer. The sea paused, taking a deep breath before it dealt the final blow, and Riley saw his chance. He let the boat ride for a second until the keel held against the sea and then he swung the boom. The mainsail filled with a cracking sound and the boat, squeezed like an orange pip between the wind and the sea, surged forward and Riley put her on course for the safety of Misterne harbour.

Bates wheeled overhead making raucous, jeering cries. Riley watched him uneasily, knowing that seagulls didn't normally behave like this one. Nothing was normal near The Sands, he should never have been persuaded to come here. Robbins raised his head from the fish boxes, where he had finally been sick. Bates streaked low, almost touching him and then was gone. Robbins waved a clenched fist after him. If he had known that Bates was Jessie's seagull, her only friend after Danny, he would have tried to fly after him. Robbins was a good reporter, there were few things he would not try. Flying was one of them.

The sea quietened as soon as they turned away from The Sands. Robbins managed a sheepish grin for Riley. "Good work," he said grudgingly. "You can certainly handle a boat." Riley grunted, but he was pleased.

"It's an unfriendly coast," Robbins said conversationally. "What did you mean when you said 'they' don't want us there?"

"I said that?" Riley glanced nonchalantly round the horizon.

"Yes, you did. Who are 'they'?"

"Just those they, that's what."

Robbins sighed. "Just-those-they-that's-what," he muttered to himself. "How can I write a report about people who talk like that?"

"That village," he said aloud, "has been under the sea for more than thirty years. You mean there are some sort of sea-ghosts of the old place still down there?"

"You saw what happened when we got close, sir."

"And you believe there's something...supernatural there?"

"I believe I nearly lost my boat. It's better you just

believe that too if I may say so, sir, and forget anything else you've heard. The Sands was always a bad place and it's best forgotten. There's no one living there now. Couldn't be. The place has been cut off from the mainland for the past nine years, you can see it has. And best it stays that way."

"Were you here when it happened?"

"Yes, sir. Man and boy I always been at Misterne."

"It must have been frightening."

"It was, sir. Like the end of the world. You wouldn't want to have something like that happen twice in a lifetime."

"What was it like?"

"Well..." Riley relaxed a little. "We knew something big was brewing. There'd been a week of gales and storms like we'd never seen before. Then this day comes, a Tuesday it was, and everything was quiet. Too quiet, you know the sort, sir, a waiting quiet, and there was something threatening about it that no one could explain. The sea was swollen, muddy looking. We just stood there on the jetty—we'd pulled the boats half-way up the street—and you know what?"

"Go on..."

*"The tide never went out that day."*

He stopped, waiting for Robbins to be impressed by his tale. He was.

"Never...that must have been...eerie."

"That's what it was, sir. Eerie. And there we all were, looking at it, waiting. Then come high water in the evening it happened. Another storm, but a real blaster this time. The water surged like the whole sea was coming up out of its bed and the land shook and thumped till we thought we were goners. We hardly knew we was still there till daylight. The lower village had been swamped and the water had gone away again, leaving great bays of shingle as far up as the graveyard. Then we saw the cliff had gone, crumbled like a piece of cake. That's how you see it today, just jagged rocks reaching out to The Sands where there used to be cliffs and fields and a road. And the sea raging round them like some monster with his tail on fire." Riley shortened sail and changed tack. He glanced at Robbins who was trying to write something on a wet piece of paper. "Now do you see, sir? No one's meant to go out there, neither by sea nor land. There's something clear as signposts saying DANGER! KEEP AWAY!" Riley smiled to himself, pleased that he had put this smart, know-all newspaperman from London in his place without being disrespectful. Robbins smiled too, because he had got someone in the strangely distrustful village to start talking for the first time.

"You know, Riley," he said smoothly, "you're an honest man. You're not afraid to put into words what other people whisper behind closed doors. I know there's a mystery here. In my line of work I often find that when something is surrounded by supposed danger, by Keep Out signs, then that's the place I want to be. That's where the story is that people ought to know."

"That's what you think, is it?" said Riley cautiously. "And what do you think they ought to know about The Sands, where no one lives and no one wants to go?"

"*If* no one lives there. I think someone does. Two people. A man, probably some mad old hermit. And a little girl. Now that's a story people should know about. That's public interest. A poor little girl imprisoned with a madman, never met another soul in the world. Our readers would want to see something done to save that little girl."

They were coming into the harbour mouth. Riley gritted his teeth and concentrated on swinging the boat at the right angle and hauling down the sails. He didn't want to hear any more from the foreigner who was creating facts out of village rumours and superstitions. He nudged the boat against the green seaweed wall of the harbour. It was mid-tide, the wall loomed above them. Usually someone came, and willing, calloused hands took his rope. Not today. They just watched in silence. Two boys fishing off the jetty glared as he went by.

People in the village turned away. Friendless months stretched ahead for Riley and he soon regretted that he had taken the newspaperman's bribe and tried to take him close to The Sands.

# Two

Danny laughed aloud as the boat disappeared, and his nightmare fears went with it. There had been boats before, smudges on the horizon, but this one had been coming deliberately to The Sands. It would never have made it, Danny knew that. But there had been a dreadful heart-stopping moment when he thought it would sink. The moment when the sea had turned vicious and he had lost sight of the boat. What would he have done then? It was a nasty question in his mind. If the boatman hadn't been so quick and experienced, if the boat had been dragged down into the village and the men were floundering in the angry sea, would he have saved them or not...

"Will they come back?" said Jessie.

"No. They must have been badly frightened."

"Oh," said Jessie, unconcerned, and she ran off.

"Where are you going?"

"To dig bait, why?"

"Later. We'll both go."

"All right," she shrugged. "I'll start the fire then."

"No. Not yet." He glanced out to sea and she understood.

"I'll go back on the dunes then, I dropped the basket when... I'll go and get it. You come too?"

Danny grinned and they raced each other into the soft sand laughing and skidding.

Danny could just remember the village, with its neat cottages and its rutted road which ran from Misterne and wound its way round the church and the inn to the wooden jetty. It was already deserted when he was a small boy because the shifting sands were in danger of smothering it. But then the sands suddenly and finally shifted inland and the sea came in to fill the gap and drowned the village. Danny remembered playing in the deserted cottages when the water was only knee-deep. By the time he was ten there was only the tip of the church steeple left above water to show there had ever been a village there at all. And then even the steeple disappeared beneath the waves.

For months, the people had been leaving. Scarcely a day passed when the road to Misterne was not dotted with plodding horses, dragging laden carts with people's homes and belongings, leaving The Sands for a safer, more solid haven. Only the oldest families remained. Tough, traditional families who had been there since the heyday of smuggling, and stayed on when that became less profitable, to fish, build boats and make nets. They had rebuilt their houses, mostly modest, two-room-and-a-store buildings, right up against the cliff when the sea took over. They were well sheltered, out of sight of Misterne, looking only towards the sea. The sea over the village developed new habits, dangerous currents, and only the hardiest seamen could venture out in their boats. The fishing industry collapsed, the carter stopped coming to transport their fish, even Smokey Sam retreated inland, leaving the vast kilns, smoke caves the Sands people called them, and the house he had built onto the rock, to its fate.

Danny and Jessie lived happily in the old kilns. It could be dank and draughty sometimes, to other people it might have seemed eerie, to them it was home. The sand still drifted in and sometimes they swept it out and sometimes they didn't bother. During winter storms they often spent days and days in the vaulted, nearly round cave where Smokey Sam had smoked his fish. It still smelt a bit fishy. They lit a driftwood fire and lay about reading, talking, telling stories, playing games, making things, mending things. The floor was covered with marram grass mats they had woven, the few bits of furniture were solid and old and had come from Danny's family and from abandoned houses in the village. The rest of the house jutted out from the cliff and stretched either side of the cave. Half the rooms were empty. One was filled with wood for the fires, another was piled high with 'Things that might come in useful one day'—bricks and chains and pieces of pipe from the old village, fish boxes and baskets that had been washed up on the beach. One room was called the Sea Store and they spent many hours in there turning the drying seaweeds they had collected to see them through the winter, powdering the ones that were already dried for the medicine cupboard or the seasoning trays.

Danny slept among his books in a huge room lined with sea chests and crates and metal boxes. "They're full of smugglers' gold," he once told Jessie dramatically. She half believed it. She knew that one of them was full of heavy old silver, another contained maps and charts and another jingled enticingly whenever Danny rummaged in it. Jessie's room was big and bright, she kept the shutters open even in the winter so that she could hear the sea. She never felt cold.

Danny was constantly putting up shelves for her treasures because she was always collecting more and never threw anything away. She had hundreds of shells of every colour and shape and size. Everything Danny had made for her since she was small had its own place. There were boats roughly made from cork floats and sailing ships delicately carved in wood and fully rigged, dolls and animals, houses, a flute, a hoop, a top...nothing was ever washed up on The Sands that Danny couldn't make into something else.

Jessie went down to the shore at each low tide to collect anything interesting that the sea had brought them. She had found Bates one day after a storm, a soggy bedraggled bundle of feathers, with his feet tangled in a length of fishing net, and one leg broken. She rushed with him to Danny who cleaned him up with warm water. "He's a black-headed gull!" said Jessie in surprise when she saw the first hint of brown summer colouring on his head. "Danny, he's just young, will he live?" Danny looked at her anxious face. When she was small she had tried to save a blinded dunlin. He had lied then, saying that it had got better and flown away. But he could not lie to her about Bates, not now, she would know.

"Silly little thing," said Danny gruffly, "getting caught at sea in a storm. He's weak, Jessie, it would be better..."

"No," said Jessie, sounding very calm and sure. "He's mine. You can't kill him. If he isn't better in the morning...then I'll do it. He's mine."

"Suit yourself," said Danny and turned away as if the bird no longer mattered. But it did matter, all birds did to him and this one more than most because Jessie wanted it. He set the gull's leg for her. Several times during the night Danny got up and crept along to Jessie's room and watched her willing the bird to live and trying to coax him to eat, and he wondered how he would comfort her when it died.

But Danny was in tears of laughter later, watching Jessie raking cockles and fighting Bates for them. She stopped, he could see her frown of concentration as she thought how to outwit him, and then he swooped and landed on her head, wrapping his wings across her face. A moment later they had both plunged into the sea and disappeared.

"Don't get used to him," Danny warned. "He's a sea bird. He'll only go back to the sea." But she had got used to him, and he stayed, and Danny was wrong for once.

Bates had been with Jessie for a whole year, she had celebrated his Coming Day just before the boat came. It was to be a secret party but Danny soon knew she was planning something, and Bates knew exactly what it was. He had already pecked at the cockle pie that Jessie had made to go with the sea beet and laver bread, he had perched on the edge of the bowl of mussels steeping in oarweed stock until it got too hot and he flew off to a rock seeming puzzled and looking at his feet.

Danny had known it was the Coming Day and he'd painted a picture of Bates sitting on the roof as a surprise for Jessie. They laughed, because they had both known what had been in each other's minds. There had never been any secrets between them, they were too close and too much together for that. After the feast, Danny drew some brandy from a cask, and he gave Jessie a drop in her hot dulse lemonade and made a little speech about Bates. He said how pleased he was that Jessie had such a fine friend in Bates, and Jessie smiled and stroked him. He nestled close to her and nibbled her ear with his beak, but when Danny came near, he stiffened and glared menacingly.

Bates had come between them, just a little bit, and not an important bit. But it was the beginning. And then the boat had come, and its coming had set them a little more apart. The nearness of other people had threatened their private world. There were questions in her mind now that had not needed answers before.

# Three

Misterne had turned its back on Robbins after his boat trip with Riley. He had had awkward times on stories before, but this, he decided, was the worst-tempered community he had ever come across. They were determined to stop him getting his story, twist and turn it as he might. He had heard strange rumours about The Sands from a friend whose cousin had stayed at the Smugglers' Loft in Misterne. The cousin had overheard a child called Lisa and an old man called Max talking about a mysterious old smugglers' lair. They had hinted that gold and treasure were stored in its caves and that a man and a girl still lived there, cut off for nine years. Robbins had checked the files from the local papers, so he knew that the land slip had completely isolated The Sands. He also gleaned a lot about its reputation because people interviewed had remembered stories of strange wrecks, sudden wealth, people disappearing never to be seen again.

Nobody remembered the stories any more, Robbins had only to mention The Sands and they clammed up on him and turned away. He felt sure they had something to hide, and they were doing it very well. He wasn't going to get his story. He wasn't going to be a hero rescuing a little girl...REPORTER RESCUES CHILD FROM MAD HERMIT...that was how he had been planning it. And there would be a tragic description of the child, thin, starved, neglected...a pitiful child who had never heard another human voice or known love or friendship...Robbins hoped he might have stumbled across some treasure out there too, and perhaps the truth about the bad old days, tales of greed and murder and intrigue, never told before...All he had got was a dangerous boat trip and a barrage of suspicion from an ignorant, superstitious village who said, if anything, "You're mad, go away! No one lives on The Sands. They couldn't. It's impossible, they must be ghosts..."

"Damn them all for liars," he said and went downstairs to the bar of the Smugglers' Loft. His arrival created a no-man's land around the bar. No one walked away deliberately, they just drifted off into little groups and eyed him warily from time to time. Ben, the landlord, wished he was a customer too and could melt away with the others. But he had to be polite. After all, the man was staying under his roof and had yet to pay the bill.

"So you've been out in Riley's boat, sir," he said roughly.

"That's right," said Robbins, deciding to bluff in the hopes that the landlord could be tricked into revealing some facts. "We got quite close to The Sands. Strange-looking place, I thought I saw something move, someone there."

"Close, were you!" said Ben, who knew better. "A

boat got close before, like a good mile out. They thought they saw things too. They didn't, of course. It's the sort of place you can imagine things that aren't there. The only thing that's real is the way the sea plays up out there, gets dangerous. Maybe you got the feeling you'd gone too far, Mr Robbins."

Robbins knew that Ben knew it all, how frightened, how sick he had been in that wretched boat.

"There must be some other way of getting there," he said, suddenly angry. "Across the land, *somehow!*"

"I told you, there's no way out there. You've seen for yourself. There's nothing but jagged rock and broken cliff where the old way used to be. And a sea boiling like a giant's cauldron you couldn't float a cork in."

"Maybe it could be done with ropes?"

"You'll have to ask George. He tried that just after the slip happened, *in case* someone had been stranded out there. But now we know that no one was. Didn't you ask George this morning? Didn't he tell you it couldn't be done?"

"I saw George all right," said Robbins grittily. "He's as blind and superstitious as the rest of you. For a policeman he's got his boots a long way off the ground."

"Keep your voice down if you don't mind," said Ben nervously because people were listening and starting to mutter angrily.

"I will not. I think there's someone out there— possibly a child in grave danger—and he should see something is done about rescuing her. I think he believes it too but he's decided to play this spooks game with the rest of you instead of doing his duty."

"Please, sir, don't make trouble..."

"I mean to make trouble. This whole village has a duty to find out about that poor mite, you're a lot of cowardly..."

"That's enough!" Ben glared round the bar. "Calm down all of you. The gentleman is leaving."

"All right," said Robbins, "but just tell me one thing. Have any of you heard the bells?"

"Bells? What bells?" There was an unpleasant silence now.

"The bells under the sea," shouted Robbins. "You're supposed to hear the bells at The Sands toll when there's a bad storm coming, when disaster is about to strike, when someone is going to die... Well? You believe in ghosts, you must have heard them..." A huge fisherman, his smock smelling of fish and his breath of beer, grabbed Robbins' cravat, twisted it and flung him out of the open door into the street. Robbins dragged himself painfully to his feet.

"You'll be sorry for this," he muttered.

"It's time you left Misterne," said the fisherman, "and tell your paper in London there's no bells can ring fifteen fathoms under the sea. Tell 'em you got it all wrong. We're peace-abiding folk here, we don't want strangers like you with your city ways coming and making trouble where none is. There's nothing for you here."

Robbins walked round the side of the Inn wishing he had trodden a little more lightly. They were a rough lot, these Misterners, but he wasn't going to give up yet. He saw Gringe practising bowls in the alley next to the Inn. He knew Gringe to be a loner, he didn't mix with the others. Gringe might be his last chance. Gringe was sweating with concentration.

"Mind if I join you?" Robbins asked in his friendly voice.

"I'm practising," said Gringe, narrowing his eyes and scowling.

"You're very good already. Very accurate. I'm staying here for a few days...lovely village you've got here...I went for a boat trip today."

"Riley took you," said Gringe, curving a bowl with perfect timing. "I heard."

"That's right. We went to The Sands, interesting place. Lonely though, ever been there?"

"No one goes there."

"Strange...I thought I saw someone...maybe a child..."

"Couldn't have done. No one there. Anyways, you wasn't close enough. You didn't get across the village even. You can't."

"Would you go there," said Robbins carefully, "if a way was found to get there?" Gringe dropped a bowl on his foot and swore.

"Would you?" asked Robbins again.

"No, I would not," said Gringe angrily. "Leave The Sands alone, it's always been a bad place. Best thing ever happened to it was the sea cutting it off from the mainland like it did."

"You mean...someone Up There," said Robbins

gesturing to heaven, "cut it off on purpose?"

Gringe faltered. "I didn't say...you're not going to write down what I been saying, for your paper, are you?"

"You haven't said anything yet," said Robbins tiredly, "but if you did...I wouldn't say it was you."

"You're trying to trick me, aren't you?" Robbins just smiled and pulled some coins out of his pocket. Gringe took a step back. "You're trying to bribe me, like you did Riley!"

"Just tell me about the girl. The one Max says is still out there."

"Max!" said Gringe, relieved. "Max is brain-sick. You can't believe anything Max says, he's mad. That's what The Sands did to him! You haven't come here because of something Max said, surely?"

"What happened to Max?" Robbins asked tersely.

"He was out there, when the slip happened. He was the only one that survived. The rest were swept out to sea and never seen again. *All of them*. Max clung to the wreckage of his boat. He got his legs smashed up, but he clung on, three days at sea...that's what did for his mind." Gringe chuckled and picked up the bowl again. "And you came all this way...you risked your life in Riley's boat...for something mad Max said! The joke's on you, mister!"

# Four

Max liked to sit in the porch of the Smugglers' Loft in the early evening. He liked the company, most people stopped to have a word with him, though few cared to get involved in his long rambling tales. Lisa did. She looked forward to the evenings when her father decided to walk down from the farmlands above Misterne to the lower fishing village. They would look at the boats and talk to the fishermen and then, as they passed the Smugglers' Loft Morgan might look thirstily at the Inn. "Go on Dad," she'd say encouragingly. "Go in. I'll be all right. I'll talk to Max."

When Lisa heard about Robbins and his pestering questions, Robbins and Riley's boat, she couldn't wait to see Max. They arrived soon after the reporter had been laughed out of the bowling alley by Gringe.

"Max! I have to talk to you!" The old man shuffled up the bench to make room for her. "What's wrong, Lisa? You look so serious!"

"It's something *very* serious," she said earnestly. "You wouldn't say anything, would you, not even if he offered you lots and lots of money?"

"Lots and lots of money? What are you saying? Who'd give mad old Max lots and lots of money?"

"That reporter, Mr Robbins, would. And you're not

mad. You're un-madder than anyone I know. You wouldn't tell, would you?" He smiled teasingly at her anxious face. "Oh! You mean, tell him about Jess..."

"Shh! Don't even say it. He might hear."

"It doesn't matter what Max says. No one believes his stories...especially about...you-know-who. They all made up their minds years ago."

"But *he*'d believe you. He'd write it all down. Max, you mustn't..."

"Calm yourself, Lisa," he said, patting her hand. "Trust me. Trust Max."

"But Max, he's going round saying...saying he *saw* someone out there, on The Sands."

"He's only saying it to try and make someone talk. He didn't see anyone, he wasn't close enough, he was too scared of the sea."

"You spoke to him? What did you say?"

Max chuckled to himself. "You'd have been proud of me, Lisa. I told him I went to sea with Lord Horatio Nelson himself and I got my legs like this on the *Victory* at Trafalgar. I told him I was captured by women pirates and..."

"Max!"

"Oh yes! And I told him that one of these women...well, that's not suitable for young ears. But it made him sit up."

"And he believed you?"

"'Course he didn't. He was getting angrier and angrier and then I made one of these faces..." Max crossed his eyes and his tongue lolled out and Lisa nearly fell off the bench with laughter.

"And then...then what did he say?"

"Something rude and he went away. So there you are, young Lisa. I wouldn't tell him about Jessie, not even for lots and lots of money." He smiled at her reassuringly and then he stared towards the sea. "I wouldn't do that," he said quietly, "Danny wouldn't like it."

They sat for a few moments silently thinking about Danny and Jessie until their thoughts were interrupted by the sound of a pony and trap rumbling up the uneven road. There were two women in it, one of them was Mrs Madden, the kindly parson's wife. The other, Lisa squirmed to see, was Miss Potter, the schoolmistress.

"It's cold," Lisa said quickly to Max. "Don't you want to come inside now and sit by the parlour fire?" Max nodded, she helped him up and they made their way into the Inn.

But Miss Potter had seen them and Miss Potter was shocked and angry.

"That child, Lisa! Going into a public drinking place! And with that dreadful old mad man Max! I shall have to do something about that!"

"You can hardly go after them, dear," said Mrs Madden practically. "I should just have a word with the girl at school tomorrow. Max isn't such a bad sort, and the child's probably lonely." Mrs Madden disappeared into a small cottage with a bundle of baby clothes from the Parish bag for a new baby. Miss Potter knew she would be there for some time, chatting and playing with the older children. She sat for a few minutes smouldering with rage. She had not been in Misterne long and she disapproved of just about everyone in it. The village was remote, backward and seemed to care little for the education of its children. The people were farming or fishing folk who smelt of the soil or the sea and thought nothing of keeping the children away from school at harvest times to work in the fields, or after storms, to help mend the nets. They wanted only that their children should follow their ignorant footsteps. It was a constant struggle for Miss Potter to persuade them to improve their minds and their manners and work towards a better way of life. What other way there might be for them, she had not properly considered.

And now this child, Lisa... Miss Potter waved her hand arrogantly at a young man who was about to go into the Inn. He looked at her just as arrogantly and then shuffled over to the trap. "You want me?"

"Yes. Be so good as to tell Mr Morgan that Miss Potter would like to speak to him. Well? You know this man Morgan?"

"Morgan? I knows Morgan right enough." Morgan came, reluctantly, accompanied by jeering because the prim, tart Miss Potter had the audacity to send for him. He tried to control his anger—she was the schoolmistress after all, and Lisa was the one who had to go to school.

"There's something the matter, ma'am?"

"Mr Morgan, this is a most improper place for a girl of Lisa's age to be at this time of day."

"Lisa?" Morgan stared at her. "Lisa's happy

28

enough, I don't see..."

"At an Inn," said Miss Potter, flustered by his hostile stare, "where rough people are taking strong drink. She should be at home...doing her embroidery...something more ladylike...don't you see..."

"No, ma'am. Lisa likes to come with me, I wouldn't leave her at home alone pretending to be a lady. Thank you for your advice."

"No, wait. You realize she's with that old madman?"

"Yes. With Max. She likes him, he tells her stories."

"Silly ghost stories, I've heard, about...about ...that *place*, out there."

"If she enjoys them there's no harm..."

"She believes them! Lisa's an imaginative child..."

"Yes," said Morgan proudly, "she is."

"It's not always a good thing here," said Miss Potter darkly. "I don't like the children making up fantasies about...about The Sands. It's just taking things that are best forgotten into another generation, isn't it?"

They looked at each other in silence for a while and then Morgan shuffled his feet. "You're a stranger here, Miss Potter. You don't know everything."

Miss Potter sighed deeply. "That poor child needs a mother," she said sadly. Morgan kicked the wheel of the trap and glared at her in fury.

"Lisa's got a father. She's got me! It's been like that since she was little. Just the two of us. I've always looked after her, she's healthy and she's happy and

I'm not asking more than that for her. You just teach her when she comes to school. I'll thank you not to interfere with what she does at home."

Morgan strode away, too angry yet to regret his temper. Mrs Madden came out of the cottage in time to catch his last words and find Miss Potter twitching with nervous fury. Mrs Madden picked up the reins and let the pony amble through the narrow streets at his own pace. It was some minutes before Miss Potter could speak.

"Insulted...dreadfully insulted," she muttered, "...that coarse, vulgar man...the things he said..."

"What did *you* say, Miss Potter?" said Mrs Madden briskly. "I did warn you not to provoke Mr Morgan."

"That child is in moral danger, I had to tell him."

"Tell him what? How to bring his daughter up?"

"Well, in a way. It's my duty."

Mrs Madden took a deep breath. It had been a mistake, appointing Miss Potter to the school. She was a distant relative of her husband, she had fallen on hard times and he had felt sorry for her.

"You must remember that you are dealing with different people now, Miss Potter. You're not a governess in a grand house any more, you're a village schoolmistress, dealing with simple country people."

"Ignorant and superstitious people..."

"They're good and honest," said Mrs Madden sharply. "They have strong family ties and it's a mistake to interfere with their home lives. Morgan's been a fine father to that girl, you know."

"Then he should have married again and provided

a proper home background for her," said Miss Potter triumphantly.

"Morgan has a wife," said Mrs Madden. "It's a pity you didn't make yourself aware of the facts. I'm sure she was a good woman," she went on, trying to be charitable, "but she'd been in service. She had fancy ideas about living in big houses, wearing beautiful clothes...being grand. Of course, she should never have married poor Morgan. She'd forgotten how to be poor, be a country girl. I'm afraid...she ran away and took up a position in a grand town house."

"Oh," said Miss Potter, taken aback briefly, and then, brightly, "Lisa should be with her mother in that case. It would be much more suitable for her."

"No, it would not," Mrs Madden said quite crossly. "You're a stranger here, Miss Potter. You must understand, Lisa belongs here, she's a country girl, she would be miserable living with her mother. Do leave well alone."

"Why were you talking to Miss Potter?"

"Maybe she just likes me," said Morgan lightly, lifting her over a stile.

"Father! She's so old and ugly!"

"Lisa! Don't speak like that about your elders."

"You were angry. I saw you being angry. Was it about me?"

Morgan smiled down at her anxious face, and flicked her hair behind her ears delicately with his big calloused thumbs. "Yes," he said, because they were always honest with each other.

"Me...and Max?" Morgan nodded. "She hates Max but I think she's really frightened of the things he says. If anyone ever talks about The Sands she goes all fluttery and her moustache quivers and...oh! Was that disrespectful?"

"Yes," said Morgan laughing, "but I've seen it happen too." They both started to giggle and then they were quiet and Lisa felt uneasy because she knew her father had something to tell her.

"Can we sit on the wall for a while? I like to see the moon come up over the sea."

"Romantic, aren't you!" said Morgan, but he stopped. There was enough moonlight now to pick out the distant line of the field and the sweep of cliff that ended abruptly where it had fallen into the sea. They could just hear the sea swirling and sucking at the jagged rocks that followed a rugged line out to sea. Out to The Sands that huddled secretly under their own cliffs, dark and massive like huge protective shoulders and arms. It seemed so tantalizingly close tonight.

"If you fired your rabbit gun from the edge of the cliff...out to sea...would the shot go as far as The Sands?"

"Nowhere near."

"Oh," said Lisa, disappointed. She jumped down from the wall. Morgan stayed still, sucking his teeth and then said suddenly, "it's your birthday next week."

"I know," said Lisa, confused by his tone. "Why are you..."

"There's a letter come from your mother."

32

"I don't want to know."

"She sent some money for your birthday."

"How much?"

"Five shillings. It's one of those post order things."

"Is that enough to buy you those boots from Mr Farthing?"

"It's for you, not me."

"I don't want it. What else?"

"She's...she's got a better position in the household," said Morgan, staring at the ground, "and the Ladyship...that is her Ladyship...says she has permission to...to send for you."

"Me?" said Lisa shocked. "Send...to *go* there ...and stay?"

"Go there and live. That's what she said."

"No! No...I live here, I don't want to go, I don't know her, I won't leave you, I won't live in a town...I don't have to, do I? You won't make me!"

"Shh! Calm down now. I had to tell you, didn't I? Of course I don't want you to go, and I wouldn't make you, ever, Lisa."

"But...*she* could make me...could she?"

"I won't let her," said Morgan suddenly hugging her roughly to hide his emotions.

They walked slowly up the hill to the farm cottage that adjoined the big barn and was so small it looked like a lean-to shed.

"Do you ever get lonely up here, Lisa?"

"No," said Lisa, startled at her father's question. "Why should I? You're here." She thought for a moment and then said accusingly, "Miss Potter said that to me. As if she wanted me to be lonely, as if there was something wrong with me because I didn't have friends my own age."

"What did you say to that?"

"I said—very politely of course—I said thank you Miss Potter but I'm quite content with my own company! And if I needed friends, Miss Potter, I could always make some up! She got very angry, her moustache did a sort of dance!"

"What's happened to all your pretend friends? They haven't been around for ages," said Morgan lightly, teasing her.

"I think they've all gone away," she said, following his banter. "Or maybe I just got tired of them."

"Even Jessie?"

"Jessie's not a pretend friend. She's just someone I haven't met—yet."

# Five

Jessie had always known that there were other people, who lived in quite different places from The Sands. She knew that some of them were quite close, yet quite remote from her life with Danny, and some of them were half a world away. Danny had made oceans and continents and mountains in the soft sand to show her what the world was like, and he had told her about them. She knew that there were vast deserts and lions in Africa and icebergs and polar bears in the Arctic Circle. Danny knew because he had gone away to sea for two years when he was young and seen many foreign places. And he read books to Jessie about famous explorers who had been to places he had not been to.

Jessie learned to read very early and she soon got tired of the picture books he found for her about little girls who lived in towns and wore pretty dresses. They were good little girls who talked to angels, or bad little girls who never went to church. Jessie practised her reading so that she could read Danny's books by the time she was seven. There were many things that puzzled her in them and she was constantly asking: "Danny? What does a stagecoach look like? Can you draw one for me, please? What does a blacksmith do? How can you get money out of a bank! That's silly!

What does this mean: 'she felt terribly lonely.' Is it like being hungry, or waiting for something to happen?"

Danny told her what it was like, living 'Inland' as he described other places away from The Sands. He spoke about it as though he and Jessie lived somewhere out at sea, where they were safe and secure, whereas those who lived 'Inland' were not. Jessie thought it sounded strange, and that people who went to buy things from shops and farms instead of finding them on the beach must have a very dull time. When she was about five, and Danny was teaching her to count with pebbles and shells, she suddenly said, "Why Danny? What does it matter how many of everything there is?"

Danny looked around for some sort of example to explain it to her.

"You need to count...oh, for lots of reasons. So that you can tell the speed of the tide, or the wind, or work out what part of the month it is, when the big tides are coming."

"They happen," said Jessie. "Whether you count them or not. Anyway, you can feel things like that, can't you."

"All right, Mistress Know-all, what about cooking? You need to count to know how long to cook a big fish or a small one. How long to boil kelp. Salt! If you want two measures of salt, you have to *count* how many measures of sea water to boil, *count* how long it will take." Jessie shook her head.

"You can tell those things. You don't need numbers."

36

"You do if you sell things and buy things."

"We don't."

"One day...you might want to, need to."

Jessie looked at him curiously.

"Is that what you do when you go away, and come back with oil and flour and things? You go to a shop, with money? You don't go pirating and smuggling?"

Danny laughed. "Is that what you thought I did? No, I go up the coast, a long way, and find a place with a harbour."

"Do you talk to people?"

"Only to ask for the things I want." He looked at her for a moment. "You've never wanted to come with me, have you, Jessie?"

"No," she said. She rather liked it when he went away, it only happened once or twice a year and she made surprises for him when he came back. And he brought surprises with him—books sometimes, and oranges, sweets or a cooking pot.

"You see...if I did take you, you might not be able to come back...people can be very nosey and interfering. They might ask where you came from and if you went to school and who looked after you..."

"Then I don't want to go. What else?"

"They might ask what happened to your mother and it would be difficult to explain."

"Why? She just went away, after I was born. What's wrong with that?" said Jessie calmly.

"One day she'll come back again for you."

"I know, you told me before."

"I don't want you to forget her."

"Maybe she'll forget to come back for me."

"No, Jessie! She loves you. She has always loved you."

"Yes, I know. Can we go down to the nets now? The tide's out."

"If you don't want to know..." She had scampered off. She never seemed to listen when he tried to tell her about her mother. Danny thought at first that she didn't want to know and it was his duty to remind her from time to time that her mother still existed. But as she got older, he realized that she knew all about her. Knew, perhaps, even more than he did.

Their life together was so simple and carefree and happy that Danny could not bear to think of it coming to an end. He hoped and prayed Jessie would not ask when that would be because he knew that it would happen in her tenth year and he did not want to start counting the weeks or months that were left.

The boat coming had been too real, it made Jessie restless. Danny's stories of people he had known, pictures of people in books—they had all seemed real enough. But they hadn't been *there*. The people in the boat had tried to come to The Sands. Friends or enemies, they were something to do with her, they had tried to form a link that had not been there before.

Everything she did now became part of that link. Even washing the clothes. It had never been important before. When their clothes seemed dirty, she or Danny took them to the freshwater stream that trickled through the rocks from a spring. They tethered them in the stream with a stone for a few hours and then laid them on the rocks to dry. Now Jessie wondered if other people in other places were doing the same thing. Did they wear the same sort of clothes? They certainly didn't in pictures in books, but Danny had explained that there were all sorts of clothes—young and old clothes, city and country clothes, rich and poor clothes. Jessie had decided that she and Danny must be very very rich because they could have as many clothes as they wanted. There were two huge trunks full of rolls of cloth, simple cottons and woollen materials, fine linen and thick rich velvets with the clear pure colours of a rock pool. The trunks had come from a wrecked ship, Danny thought it was French, he couldn't remember now.

Danny had made Jessie's clothes when she was small, little skirts and bodices, roughly cut with a knife and stitched with thick thread. The seams bulged and chafed and she often threw them off and wrapped herself in a length of cotton.

During the winter of her seventh year, she found a wooden box washed up on the shore after a gale and rushed with it to Danny.

"It's a lady's box," he said excitedly. "Probably belonged to a soldier's wife going out to India...Look, Jessie! Now you can be a grand lady...look!"

Jessie had laid all the things out on the beach and puzzled over them. A little oval picture, a mirror and a leather pouch of necklaces and brooches, a carved shoe horn. Then she found a leather case with some fine needles, a thimble, some scissors and some unfinished embroidery. She cleaned the rust off the needles and the scissors with sand and taught herself to sew neat little stitches that didn't bunch or even show.

"Danny? What do you think?"

"Turn round... how did you know?"

"Know? Know what? I made it, Danny. With the fine lady's needles. Isn't it nice?"

"Yes."

"I just took a piece of cloth and doubled it...and made a hole for my head...stitched the sides...see how it flows, like water?"

"Yes. And you caught it up with a sash...so it falls in...folds...like...like a goddess. Did you copy it, from my book...about heroes and..."

"No, Danny! I just did it!" There was something wrong. "You don't like it, do you? Why not? Why don't you? I did it myself, I thought you'd like it!"

"Put a shawl on. You'll be cold."

"I threw my shawl away."

"Make another. There's plenty of woollen cloth."

"I'm not cold, Danny. Feel."

She held out her hand and he took it and tried to smile at her before he walked away.

*She was cold and she was beautiful and now she was dressed like Mara.*

Jessie went on making her dresses in the same way, they were comfortable and she felt right in them. She learned to make smocks for Danny, too.

She was pleased and didn't think any more about clothes until the boat came. The men on it had only been specks against the sails. She would have liked to know what they looked like, what they wore, whether they smiled. And then she realized that they would have looked at her as well. She wondered what it would feel like, being looked at. And what would other people see?

If they spoke, would they sound like Danny?

For the first time she tried to listen when she spoke to herself.

Danny said the boat would not come back, the sea had spelt out its warning. But its coming remained, like the memory of an unsettling dream. She wanted a storm to come and wash it away, she liked storms, they thrilled her. But there was no storm on the horizon, there was nothing, nothing. She watched the sky at night, waiting for the moon to come back and bring the big tides. Danny watched her watching and waiting. She had always been quiet during the neap tides and the waning moon, her moods changed with the tides as if she needed the pull of the moon's force to give her life. Danny knew that. But now she was especially tired and listless. She watched the sluggish water rising and falling only a few yards and scarcely talked to Bates who was dropping a mussel on the rocks beside her, trying to crack the shell.

The tide's reach lengthened again and Jessie felt better at once. Her energy returned as she ran playing with Bates on the wet sand, and fishing with him for crabs and winkles, cockles and mussels in pools that had not been uncovered for months. Jessie perched on a rock near the old village road staring out to sea. It was the lowest spring equinox she had ever seen and the tide was still ebbing.

"Bates!" she said with alarm, "it isn't going to stop. It's going out and out forever!" It was suddenly a very eerie possibility, the sea retreating, leaving the undulations of the sea bed, its mountains and valleys exposed, stretching away for ever. And the village, its bare, sea-smoothed walls dripping, gleaming in the watery sun. Jessie could see the faint remains of the old road; it crept out from underneath the fallen cliffs on Boulder Beach and ran haphazardly until it straightened and plunged into the sea. Jessie could picture the village very clearly now in her mind. She sat so still and concentrated so hard that she could even hear it. A village waking up on a clear winter morning. Dogs barking, a barrow's iron wheels grating on the cobbles. Doors opening, people coming out, sea boots walking away, mats being shaken...a baby crying, children chasing each other over the church wall, women calling out to each other.

The noises faded and Jessie laughed to herself to think she had heard them and known what they were. She started to build in the sand, and didn't notice when the tide turned.

Much later Danny came along the beach swinging two crabs in a piece of net. Jessie went to take them from him, but he laughed and hid them behind his back.

"They're huge! Shall I do them?"

"No, Jessie, not today."

"Why not today?"

"You've forgotten? It's March, didn't you notice the tide?"

"The first quarter of the moon!" said Jessie excitedly. "The spring equinox...my birthday!" Danny dropped the crabs and lifted her high in the air, confusing Bates. "Happy Birthday, Jessie! You really had forgotten, hadn't you!"

"I really had! But you didn't...have you...have you done something special?"

"You'll see," said Danny enjoying himself in anticipation. He looked down at the sand, idly at first and then intrigued. "What have you been making?"

"The village. The village under the sea."

Danny put her down gently.

"You've made the village," he said slowly.

"Yes," said Jessie proudly. She knelt down beside it again. "That bit's wrong isn't it, by the jetty, the road bends this way...and then there's an odd-shaped house on the corner...here...like that!"

"It was a barn," said Danny automatically, "they dried the nets in there when it was raining..."

Jessie sat back on her heels and surveyed it with her head on one side.

"Do you like the Inn? And those two funny little cottages by the place where they weighed the fish?" She frowned and knocked the steeple off the church and made it again, taller. "There! That's better!" She looked up at Danny, expecting him to be pleased and impressed.

"How did you know?"

"Know? Know what? Danny? What's wrong?"

"How did you know what the village was like?"

"I just...what's the matter? Have I got it wrong?"

"No. You've got it exactly right," said Danny, puzzled, "but how did you know it was like that?"

"I've been there. You must have taken me there ages ago. When I was small."

"It was under the sea, long before you were small."

"Well, I must have been there *sometime*, or I wouldn't remember it, would I?" She jumped up, smacking the sand off her legs. "What are you going to do with the crabs?"

"Secret," said Danny, taking her hand. "They'll be very tasty, you'll see."

They walked along the shoreline, kicking up the surf. The tide was coming in swiftly now after its great drop, putting out foamy fingers into Jessie's village. She looked back and saw the church melt and wash away.

"Maybe I dreamt going to the village," she said lightly.

"Maybe you did. You're a great dreamer."

"Do you know what I dream about?"

"No. Dreams are...well, secrets to the dreamer because they happen inside your head."

"Sometimes I know what's happening inside your head."

"Oh yes? You didn't know I'd been thinking about your birthday though, did you?" Jessie laughed. "No, I didn't. But I know sometimes when things make you

sad...even when you just dream them at night."
Danny picked up a stone and made it jump five times
through the waves.

"Danny, can you hear things in dreams?"

"Yes," said Danny and then thought and shook his
head. "No. Not really. You think you hear things, but
there isn't really any sound. No one else would hear
it."

"I heard the church bells though. That wasn't a
dream."

"*When?*" His voice cracked like a whip and made
Jessie jump.

"You're angry. Danny, why?"

"I'm not angry. I asked when?"

"You're angry, you are! Like when I went on
Boulder Beach. You were angry then!"

"Yes. Then. It was dangerous. I was afraid for you.
Afraid you might get hurt, I told you that. I'm not
angry now!"

"You are. You're shouting at me. And it's my birthday! You've gone all fierce like...like Bates gets with
you!"

They were staring at each other, like two fighting
gulls. They knew it was wrong. They had never been
like this with each other before.

"Come here, Jessie," Danny whispered contritely.
She went towards him slowly, her feet scuffing the
sand clumsily. He slipped his rough fisherman's hands
under her hair, hooked it back over her ears. "Did you
really hear the bells?"

"Yes," she said, feeling guilty, wanting to lie. "Yes,

45

I did. Not just once. Twice or more. It was a long time ago, but I remember. Why does it matter?"

"It doesn't. Forget it." He hugged her roughly and pushed her away.

"Go and rinse your hair," he said in a different voice. "It's all sticky with salt."

"All right, Danny," she said, feeling it. "And I'll plait it, for my birthday, yes?"

"Yes!" Danny was suddenly pleased. Tonight he did not want to see it blowing in the wind. "Yes!" He watched her run through the surf and suddenly veer off up the beach towards the stream with Bates ducking and swooping around her. He cupped his hands to shout after her. "If you hear the bells again, don't listen!" She cupped her hands back, "What?"

"Don't listen!" Danny shouted into the wind that rushed his voice away. "Cover your ears. Don't listen to them." Jessie waved as if she had heard and was gone. "Please don't listen to them, Jessie. Not unless you have to. Pretend you can't hear them, stay with me."

# Six

"Stay here, Jessie." Danny glanced round, looking for a place to anchor time. "Stay here until the sun is behind the Sentinels."

Jessie smiled and nodded. They had put aside their morning differences, it was afternoon now, Jessie's birthday afternoon.

"Yes, Danny. Then what?"

"Then follow the trail!" he shouted dramatically.

"Trail?"

"You'll find it," said Danny laughing and setting off, dragging the sand sled made from fish boxes and driftwood and mounted on barrel hoops.

Jessie wandered round the kilns looking for things to do. It was unusual for her because most days she did things that needed doing. Sweeping out the sand, turning the seaweed, fetching water, gathering driftwood. There was no pattern, no time, no urgent need. She did what she felt like doing, Danny did the same. But now, something was going to happen. Her birthday was going to happen. She had to wait because it would happen at a certain time. When the sun went down. It was a long way from the Sentinels. She wanted to reach out to the sun and push it down with her arms into the sea.

47

She went up the rickety wooden steps to the look-out Danny had built over the entrance to the kilns. It was a long thin room built from old ships' timbers which gave it an odd shape. There were shutters across the front which could all be taken out in good weather, and then it was rather like being on a ship. Jessie opened some of them now to let the light in and Bates perched on one, cocking his head comically to see what Jessie was doing.

"Stay like that," she said, "I'll draw a picture of you." She chose one of Danny's newly sharpened quills and dipped it into the bottle of cuttle-fish ink that Danny said people called sepia. Bates flew away. "Come back, Bates, and be drawn," called Jessie but he had found something in the rubbish pit by the Sea Store. She tried to write a poem about him instead but the words wouldn't come and she washed the quill and put it back with the others. The sun was no closer to the Sentinels. She thought it had stopped moving and just hung there in the sky laughing at her impatience.

She leafed through some of Danny's drawings. They were mostly of birds, he spent hours just watching birds and then drawing them. He drew sea-flowers too, and carved pictures on cuttle-bone. Jessie picked up one of these and held it to the light, wondering how he, with his big blunt fingers, could carve something as delicate as fine lace when her thin, nimble fingers could barely outline a ship without breaking it.

The sun had dropped a finger's width closer to the rocks. Jessie tried not to keep looking at it. She lifted Danny's heavy log book down from a shelf. It was like a ship's log—he made notes about the tides and the winds, bird patterns, seaweed patterns, points on the beach where the tidewrack changed or different types of flotsam and jetsam were washed up. Jessie had only recently understood how important all these things were to the changing shape of The Sands. Danny kept detailed charts to show how the shoreline changed, currents changed direction, new sand banks appeared, old ones shifted dramatically. He always took them with him when he went out in the boat, even if it was just a little way to fish. He had drawn sketches for Jessie, too. She mulled over them now. Ten years ago the solid mass of cliff had formed a wide sweep of bay for The Sands, and then swept back in an arc to join the cliffs near Misterne. But Danny's detailed sketch from the following year looked like a different place altogether. The arc of the cliff had gone and there was just a clutter of jagged rocks and boulders following the line it had taken. The long smooth bay had gone and it was now a series of inlets. Boulder Beach was all that remained of the last settlement at the bottom of the cliff. The boulders, some as big as houses, stretched out to sea and sheltered the next new bay, where Danny and Jessie lived, from the worst storms. It was these boulders that had changed the pattern of the sea and made it so dangerous near the sunken village. Only Danny had the charts to steer a safe course through them. The bay near the kilns, now protected, had grown, there were new areas of sand, new dunes had formed and new shore plants held them together. At the far end there was a headland which now stood out prominently and the changing sea patterns were constantly throwing up shingle and changing the shape of the shore. Jessie put the sketches away carefully in a map-roll. The sun had moved another finger and Bates had come back and left a splat of droppings on Danny's papers.

"Filthy bird," said Jessie crossly. "You did that on purpose!" She sighed and tried to clean it up. "Why can't you be nice to Danny? Why?"

Danny's bird records were badly smudged. He was making lists of all the new birds that had come to The Sands in the last ten years, the new plants that had been established by birds dropping the seeds, the new seaweeds that the currents washed in. Jessie decided she would copy out the page, very beautifully, as a surprise for Danny. She privately thought that her writing, like her sewing, was much neater than his. She was so engrossed with her labour that the next time she glanced up the sun was already touching the Sentinel rocks, flushing them a warm pink.

"Now," she yelled, hurtling down the rickety stairs. "Now Bates!"

Danny had written HAPPY BIRTHDAY JESSIE in huge letters across the beach. She ran along the trail left by the sled, looking carefully to each side of it for signs or arrows that led to a rock pool or a clump of reeds or samphire in the shingle. In each hiding place she found a little present wrapped in cloth. This year he had made even more and better presents than ever, she gathered them up carefully and ran laughing towards the smoke and the cooking smells that showed her where Danny had chosen for her birthday celebration this year.

The soup was steaming enticingly on the hot embers of driftwood, underneath the sand the crabs were baking, wrapped in clay from Boulder Beach. Danny grinned with delight at Jessie's pleasure. She grinned back, laying the presents he had made neatly around the cairn of stones he had set up. Nine stones this year, poised, insecurely it seemed, one on top of the other, yet so chosen and placed that they would stand up to the fiercest winter gales. Her other birthday stones still stood solidly in different parts of The Sands. Jessie often went to visit them, they were important to her. She knew that if ever one of them fell down, she would be afraid. Her faith in Danny was as firm as that. Danny always built them well above the highest tide level so that the sea could not reach them

He had another present for her this year. It dangled on a chain from his fingers, a crude, silvery figure, blunted with age. It glinted, reflecting the fire, but its light was cold. Like moonlight. Jessie shuddered and took a step back.

*I don't think I want it, Danny. Don't give it to me...not yet...*

"Are you going to put it on? Jessie?"

She looked at his disappointed face and reached out her hand slowly.

"Yes. In a minute." She put it down carefully on a stone.

"You don't like it."

"Yes. Yes, it's...beautiful, Danny. Thank you."

Danny turned away from her to stir the soup. "It's your mother's," he said gruffly. "You're in your tenth year. I thought...thought..."

"I know," said Jessie evenly. "It's her Salacia."

"Her what?"

"Salacia," said Jessie, churned with confusion because Danny did not understand. "Her goddess of the salt seas. She left it behind for me."

They both turned at once and reached for the same piece of wood to throw on the fire. They laughed then. The fire crackled and the crabs were ready. It was Jessie's birthday. Danny's party. Nothing must change that. They ate greedily and licked their fingers and played pebble games. They told each other stories and sang some of Danny's full-blooded sea songs.

The fire burned down and the moon came up. They lay sprawled in the sand on either side of the embers. Danny gazed at the last red firelines making erratic patterns. Jessie stared at the white moonlight quivering on the dark sea. They were apart now. Danny felt the distance between them growing and aching. Jessie's birthday was over. She was in her tenth year. He knew she was changing. She's older, wiser, he thought. She knows things that I do not know. She goes to places in her mind where I cannot go. It's all part of a pattern. Oh God! Why can't I stop it. Why did I give her that goddess thing? *Why didn't I know it would take her closer to Mara?*

Jessie caught his mood and it made her feel guilty because she had hurt him. She had never wanted to have secrets from him. She didn't want them now—

knowing about Salacia, hearing the bells, seeing the village so clearly.

"Danny," she said suddenly. "What will you do on my birthday next year?" Danny stared deeper into the fire and could not answer.

"I won't go!" She had jumped to her feet and was staring at him with wild frightened eyes. "I won't, Danny, I won't!"

So she knew. Or she guessed. Danny tried to reach out to her. "Jessie, when the time comes, when it happens..."

"It won't happen. I won't let it happen. I just won't go when my mother comes back, I'll say No! I'm not coming! I'm staying here with Danny!"

He let her go and sob her rage and frustration into the sand. He longed to comfort her, tell her that he understood that she was being pulled apart by two quite different forces. But he didn't understand, he couldn't. He picked up the little image he had given her and waited for her to come back.

"Better?" Jessie nodded, feeling ashamed.

"You mustn't cry. You'll understand when the time comes and you'll want to go."

"It's you..."

"I know how to be alone. You must never cry for me. Promise me that. Promise?"

"Do I have to?"

"Yes. Now smile for me. That's better." He held up the chain and the Salacia swung between them. "I'll take this back if you like."

"No." She knelt in the sand and he slipped it over

53

her head and loosened her hair around it. "Shall we build up the fire again?"

"No. It's too hot. Let's go and swim in the sea."

"Certainly not! It's freezing cold."

"No, it isn't. I must go. Come with me, Danny."

"No. Don't go, please."

"Yes. Come?"

"I'll come and stand by the shore." Jessie ran ahead of him struggling out of her dress as she ran.

"Come back soon," Danny called after her, but she was just a distant pale figure, her hair streaming behind her. Soon there was nothing but the dark sea.

The surf was making white frills against Danny's sea boots. The cold was reaching through them, chilling his feet painfully. He stamped up and down on the shore and thought about going back to rekindle the fire, or going back to the kilns and his bed. But he had promised Jessie he would wait. He was not afraid for her.

The moon arched overhead, the waves pounded relentlessly beating their ancient rhythm on the shore. The cold dark beach reminded Danny of years gone by, when his father and his friend Max ran the smuggling on this part of the coast. Danny remembered boats with muffled oars sneaking to the shore without lights. And the villagers who still remained, men, women and sturdy children, filtering down to meet the boats and heave the crates and barrels up to Elder's Cave. There had been tense excitement in the air. Danny was often posted as a look-out for the coastguards, it was an adventure because he was young and he was allowed to stay out at night, and be useful.

Old people, crippled with rheumatism in their sea-gnarled joints, chafed at home and told tales of the bad old days. Danny remembered, when he had been considered too young for their tales, creeping down at night to listen at the door. He had been chilled with fear to hear of ships being lured onto the Sentinels and wrecked. Of people being killed in cold blood, of feuds with coastguards, of villagers greedily fighting among themselves.

"Was The Sands really such a wicked place?" he whispered once to his mother. She had slapped him soundly, once for listening at the door and again for being afraid of what he heard. Then she had hugged him and grinned. "Yes. The Sands have always been wicked as sin with men to match. Thank God for that!"

Danny swung his arms round him to try and ease the pain of the cold in his hands. The moon had gone, thin fingers of daylight were filtering through the clouds, changing the landscape. Jessie had still not come back.

# Seven

Robbins had finally given up and gone back to London, muttering darkly about the unfriendly people of Misterne.

Lisa was relieved. His presence had been a threat to Danny and Jessie and she had felt nervous and apprehensive all the time he had been snooping around. She didn't want anyone else to know about Jessie. She wanted to keep her to herself. And Max, of course.

"How old would Jessie be now?" she asked him one Sunday morning when she had found him sitting on a bench by the sea wall, wrapped in sacks. Max sucked his gappy teeth noisily and thought hard.

"Round and about the same age as yourself, I'd say."

Lisa was pleased. It was something else she could share with Jessie. "I'm nearly nine," she said. "My father's got me something special for my birthday. It came on the carter's wagon last week and it's under his bed. Miss Potter lets us all choose a hymn to sing on our birthdays. Then everyone knows whose special day it is. Poor Jessie. She wouldn't have a proper birthday would she, with no shops and no school and just Danny?"

"Why wouldn't she now?" Max sounded grumpy,

he was pulling back into his shell like a tortoise. Lisa thought he looked rather like one with his grey scaly neck and his watery eyes. He even had skin so thick and weather-coarsened you could probably knock on it and hear an echo.

"Celebrate anything, would Danny in the old days," he said, still grumpy. "Always liked a party until...but anyway, why wouldn't he make a birthday for his Jessie? Eh?" He closed his eyes and faced the sun which was beginning to have some warmth in it. Max could be possessive about The Sands. Lisa knew she had to be careful what she said and not surprise him by asking about present-day things. He thought about The Sands the way it had been, not the way it was now. The past was a special place to him. It had to be treated with care.

"The newspaperman's gone away," Lisa said to change the subject. Max nodded.

"You know Mrs Crane's mother, old blind Rose...she said he really came after Danny's gold!"

"Danny's gold?" Max snorted and then he laughed, a real full-throated laugh that made the tears run down the wrinkles on his face.

"Other people said so too," said Lisa indignantly. "They said it was obvious no one could still be living there so it must have been some sort of treasure. Max...is there really treasure out there...and secret passages...and pirates' swords and chests of gold coins?"

Max controlled his laughter and wiped his eyes with a grimy rag.

"It's all right, girl," he said, seeing her anxious face. "Just makes me laugh when folks talk of The Sands being...romantic...swashbuckling...especially after all the bad, dead things they've been saying about it for years. Let them believe what they want to believe, I'll talk no more about it now."

"You will to me, won't you?"

"You? You're just a scrap of a girl..."

"But I believe you, Max. I don't think you carry the wickedness of The Sands with you."

"I'd heard they said that," said Max thoughtfully. He paused. "Treasure! So you want to know about treasure. Well, plenty of treasure passed through The Sands in my father's day. and gold...and much more besides. Maybe some got stuck on the way. I shouldn't wonder Danny didn't keep a few trinkets. But that's going back a bit. Me and Danny's father, we smuggled brandy and tobacco mainly. That's where the money was after the wars. Besides, the coastguards were getting wise, they were better trained, armed. Treasure! I remember the time Danny's mother lifted him out of his babby cot and under the mattress there were guns packed tight as a shoal of herrings. If it were ever romantic, it had stopped, it was a hard life for hard people."

"Was there a secret passage?" Lisa waited, hoping and hoping.

"'Course there was. How do you think we'd have got the stuff past the customs officers? It was a long one and a dangerous one, especially the bit they called Dead Man's Walk."

"Max...is it still there? Could you still get out to The Sands?"

Max smiled, deep inside himself so that only a chink of the smile showed in his sea-faded eyes.

"There is! Isn't there!"

"If there was...Max'd be the one to know. No, Lisa, it's gone now, must have gone. When those cliffs came down they came down for good and who's to say if it was an accident or if the sea chose to cut The Sands off for ever. Think about it, girl, and maybe you'll think twice about wheedling Max into taking you out there, for I know that's in your mind. I couldn't go, not with these cripplin' legs of mine. No! There is no way."

Lisa knew she had gone too far and angered Max. She also knew deep down that she didn't want there to be a way, not for anyone, not even for herself because she wouldn't be welcome in Danny and Jessie's life. If Jessie found it...if Jessie came...It would have to be soon. She didn't know why, only that she was sure. Jessie was so close and so very far away.

"I wish I'd been born on The Sands," she said casually, hoping to start Max up again, like bowling her hoop down the incline towards the harbour.

"I wish I'd been born a smuggler's daughter. Did they have girl smugglers?"

Max chuckled to himself. Lisa waited, he was on the incline...

"Girl smugglers! Ahh! They were some of the best. I can see them now, barefoot on the rocks, moving like cats when we were slipping around in sea boots. Saints alive! How they could turn a half-anker cask in the air

59

lifting it down from a boat. Their skirts swirling, lifting in the waves. Men didn't like them doing it, being so good..." He stopped and drifted away in his mind. Lisa prayed he had not stopped, she daren't speak. When he started again he was talking for himself, not to her.

"Young lass, climbing the Sentinels from a boat at dead of night. Just like a little sure-foot mouse climbing a haystack...Danny's mother, she was one could do it, carrying a lamp that weighed like a rock itself. Right up to the top and set it down. Shone out like a beacon...Danny wasn't born then, of course. She'd not have risked it with one in the cradle."

Lisa was shocked, but thrilled too. "Then it's true, it's all true about The Sands!"

"What?" Max started, as if he had just woken up.

"It's true about the wreckers. There were wreckers...luring ships onto the rocks, killing people, wrecking ships and taking the spoils from the wreckage. That's why The Sands were so bad!"

"Bad?" Max smiled at her shocked face. "No...The Sands weren't really a bad place." He looked dreamily out to sea, going back to The Sands in his mind.

Below on the beach a small child dragged a long-dead fish over the shingle. Across the harbour wall masts bobbed and ducked with the rising tide. In the village above a horse moved restlessly, creaking its harness. There was a shout followed by the grinding of wheels on a rough road and the hollow thud of the horse's feet.

"Wrecking's wicked though, isn't it, Max?" Lisa

said reproachfully because she didn't want The Sands to be really sinful.

"Wrecking? Now Lisa I didn't say...anyway it was before the lighthouse came to Misterne. That stopped any goings on...we were just honest smugglers."

"Isn't smuggling wrong? Like stealing?"

"Bless you no. It's...trading in a manner of speaking. Providing goods that people who *has* money can buy and those who *hasn't* can make a bit of a living passing them on." Max waved angrily back at the village. "This place—a poor village it was—thrived on smuggling. There wasn't a family, little children up, couldn't make a few pence doing look-outs, portering...not a farmer didn't hire his wagons out or his barns...no one could live off the land, not in those days. They couldn't have lived without the men—and the lasses—at The Sands doing all the hard and dangerous work for them!"

"I didn't know that," said Lisa, quietly pleased.

"No. And the villagers have all chosen to forget. They got no rights to go saying harsh words about The Sands now, saying there's wickedness lives on...not after what it did for them. They had it easy, we had it hard. We had the seas against us, the coastguards, the revenue cutters, the riding officers...the greedy venturers. It was a life for those who didn't need friends. You made enough enemies."

Max turned away from Lisa abruptly. Lisa looked thoughtfully at the back of his head. Danny didn't need friends, Jessie wouldn't need friends...she felt strangely proud of them both.

# Eight

Jessie came back at dawn, moving effortlessly through the water, with Bates wave-hopping beside her. It was not until she struggled to her feet in the surf that she faltered with exhaustion. Danny ran to catch her, she smiled wanly up at him and then her eyelids flickered and closed.

He carried her back along the smudged birthday trail. It had been fun preparing it for her the day before but in the cold morning light it just seemed childish and silly. Jessie was years older than she had been yesterday.

Danny watched her sleeping, not stirring from the position in which he had laid her on her bed. He spread her hair out to dry on the pillow. She looked pale and peaceful, there were strands of yellowy green seaweed caught up in the chain around her neck.

He knew what he would do next. He would show her that there was a way out of The Sands. She must have a chance to go Inland if she wanted to, while there was still time.

At the back of his mind he had a pang of guilt that he was somehow cheating Mara. He pushed it away. If there was something about Inland, someone perhaps, some force that might change her, keep her...then it would be Jessie's choice.

He left her sleeping and strode down the beach to Elder's Cave, where they kept the boats. They were stranded now on the ebbing tide, leaning over in the sand. The cave was deep and only a faint light filtered through to the back. Danny remembered how scared he had been as a boy when he had first gone there. His mother had sent him with an urgent message for his father. It had been nearly dark, he had hesitated at the entrance because the sea monster was supposed to have a lair in Elder's Cave. The Sands children were always frightening each other with tales of the monster and Danny still thought then that they were true.

He had heard it, that first time. A distant screech and groaning noise that made him back away in terror. He might have run home, leaving his father to the sea monster, but Max had come along just in time. He had taken him into the cave, laughing at his fears and showing him where the pulleys screeched and groaned swinging crates and barrels into a dark gaping hole which was the entrance of the secret passage through the cliffs to Misterne. The rope-ladder for the men to climb was still there. Danny felt his way into the niche where it was kept and heaved it down. It was stiff with salt and hung in angled kinks until Danny put all his weight on it. It still held.

He climbed up. It smelt danker than ever and it was very cold. He could find his way easily in the dark, he knew every bend and slant and wickedly jutting rock edge. But he went cautiously in case any new rock falls had taken place since he last checked it.

# Nine

Max came out of his doze with a little snort. "What were you saying?"

Lisa thought quickly, they had been talking about not needing friends when he'd dropped off.

"Not having friends at The Sands," she said. "Didn't Danny ever *like* anyone even?"

"Danny? Course he did. Young Danny! He was wild as a lad. Went off to sea and saw a fair bit of the world. But he came back, he had to come back. Came back a man, big, wide, strong, like his Dad. With his looks too, eyes like bits of summer sky that could break a young girl's heart. We always said when they gave out the looks on The Sands they gave 'em all to Danny and his son."

"Did he have lots of...lady friends?" said Lisa cautiously.

"Young Danny? Come to think of it...no, not that I knew of. There was just...just the one. There was always a bit of a loner in Young Danny, and then when Old Danny went, then he got to be a real loner."

"Where did Old Danny go?"

Max looked far away and so melancholy that Lisa was afraid she had jolted him with her question. Old Danny had meant a lot to him.

"He went out in his boat one night, and he came back without it," said Max suddenly and abruptly. "He never learned to swim. A lot of seamen don't. They reckon it leads to a lot of drownings. You're best clinging to the wreckage, see? Only this time they made sure there wasn't any wreckage. I know that, I spent a time looking for it."

"You mean...he was..."

"Tch! I told you. You could always make enemies out there. Greed makes enemies out of friends, enemies in families even. It was never healthy to get rich on The Sands."

"Then...he *was*...for his gold!"

"No one ever said that, girl. But he wouldn't have been the first. I've known plenty die before their time. Young Danny knew though. Nothing he could do about it but he didn't have time for people after that. His mother came Inland and it soon did for her."

"Then what did he do? Young Danny?"

"Went on. Bit of fishing, mending boats...he could turn his hand to anything. There weren't many people left then. Danny moved into the old kilns, great ramble of a place, just him and his books. Hundreds of books he must have had. We always made fun of Danny and his books. Most of us couldn't read...but to Danny, books were like friends. He learned things from them we didn't know about. Things we couldn't start to understand. With the village going the way it did, there wasn't much learning so it put Danny apart somehow. That did. And then there was his woman. Then there was Mara."

65

Lisa almost held her breath, she daren't move. Max was gazing out to sea as if he was in a trance, back there at The Sands, young again. He had never spoken about Jessie's mother before...he mustn't, *mustn't* be put off now. Mara! So that was her name!

"Mara," said Max, repeating it like a charm, "Mara! She was beautiful, Lisa, really beautiful. You could wonder sometimes how it was she walked on the same earth that you did. She was just like a goddess and I was a befuddled old fool who could have fallen at her feet and worshipped her. Hm! Everything...*flowed* about Mara, her long fair hair, the strange dresses she wore...just simple dresses but so graceful...She'd walk along the shore and they'd flow round her like water. She loved to sing, strange haunting melodies we'd never heard before. I'd give the rest of my life to hear them again." There were tears in his eyes. Lisa felt a lump in her throat, she hoped she would not cry and embarrass him but the thought of the ugly old man breaking his heart over a beautiful young woman was so pitiful...

"Where did she come from?" Lisa asked unsteadily.

Max was silent and for a terrible moment Lisa was afraid she had broken the spell, there would be no more about Mara.

"She came," he said at last. "She just came and she was there and no one ever knew. Some asked Danny. He just laughed and said she had come from the sea one dark night. Maybe he was jealous, he wouldn't talk about her. There was gossip of course, she had to have come from somewhere. Some thought she'd come

66

from a ship at sea. Some said he'd taken her from an island far off the coast, or he'd captured a rich man's daughter...she had a sort of style like she could have been rich. We never found out. But the night she came, there was a storm such as we'd never seen before. No man, not even Danny, could have taken a boat out that night."

"Then she really came from the sea?" breathed Lisa.

Max nodded. "And I reckon Danny knew she'd go back there one day, after her baby was born. Maybe it was the night of the storm. The night the cliffs fell in. The bells were ringing then, all right."

"Max! Was she...was she a...*mermaid*?"

"Mermaid? Mara?" Max started to laugh in great rolling chuckles. Lisa wished he would stop. She hadn't said anything funny. It was something she had thought about ever since she had read some stories about mermaids. In the stories they did lure mortal men into the depths of the sea. And sometimes they came on land with them and they took human form and had human souls...for a time. Not for long. Then she remembered that in all the stories, they brought grief and suffering to the mortal man.

"Max, *really*...you said she was different...she could've been!"

"Mermaid indeed, one of them with fish tails and long hair sitting on the rocks? Mara had legs I'll swear to that. When she tucked up those skirts to dig for lug worms she had the finest pair of legs ever graced The Sands. Mermaid!" He stopped to wipe his eyes and saw Lisa's hurt expression. He had shattered her dreamworld, he had not meant to do that.

"You're right, she was no ordinary woman. People were afraid of her."

"Afraid? Why?"

"She walked alone, sometimes at night, singing those haunting songs...not quite alone, she had a sea-gull that was always with her. Just an ordinary gull but it stayed with her and seemed to hate everyone else, even Danny, and he had a way with birds. No, that bird never left her...people said it was...her 'familiar'—you know? Like a witch has a cat. She knew a lot of ancient folklore. She used to brew up potions and medicines out of seaweeds and sand plants, cured a few ills with them too. But people said she might...you know—use them the other way if you crossed her. She never ate things that didn't come from the sea or the shore. She taught Danny that. To live off the sea, off the shore."

Lisa smiled and nodded rather smugly. It was part of the Misterne argument that no one—no flesh-and-blood-person—could live on The Sands. What would they eat? Seaweed? Nonsense! Now she knew better.

"I'm tired now, Lisa," Max said. "Tired of talking. Said too much anyway...don't you go telling anyone what I've told you. They say I'm mad. They say I shouldn't talk about things that don't exist, say it's dangerous to make things up that frighten people."

"But you don't..." Lisa watched him sleeping. A tatty old bundle tied in the middle with a frayed piece of rope. An ancient sea tramp washed up on a hostile shore. Surely he didn't make things up, did he? She knew he got things wrong sometimes because he was old. She had suspected sometimes he had embroidered some of his stories for her benefit. Told her things she wanted to hear because he thought she was lonely.

But not Jessie. He couldn't have made up Jessie for her. Jessie had to be real. But how would she ever know?

Not believing in Jessie, being like everyone else in Misterne, that would be worse than...than...she couldn't think of anything worse that would be bearable.

# Ten

When Jessie woke up she was mystified to find that it was dark and she had lost a whole day. Bates was waiting impatiently on her windowsill, hopping on his uneven legs. He had spent a boring day waiting for her to wake up. She found Danny getting the supper ready and wrinkled her nose nervously.

"Hullo, Danny."

"Hullo, Sleeping Beauty!" He picked her up with one arm and hugged her to him. His other arm was stirring the supper over the fire.

"You're all right, are you?" There was nothing else he could ask her.

"Yes, thank you. Danny...please don't be cross...but..."

"But what?" He looked at her staring into the steaming pot and she felt him stiffen slightly.

"I don't want to eat fish any more."

"That's all right," he said gently. "I'm not cross. Go and get some more sea beat and kale or you'll be hungry."

He didn't tell her about the way out that night. She was sweet and amusing as usual but he could see underneath she was worried and he couldn't un-worry her.

It happened a few days later. The moon was waning, the tides were lethargic again and so was Jessie. Danny watched her sitting on the shingle, doing nothing, absolutely nothing. She had never done that before. Later she took a knife and went down and cut her nets away and let them drift out with the tide. She had had her own nets since she was small, she had always run down eagerly at low tide to see what fish she had caught, and run back to show it to Danny.

He told her then about the way out. At first she was angry because she had not known about it before. Then she was angry because now she knew and she did not know what to do about it. Finally she was angry because Danny wanted her to go. She went off with Bates into the sand dunes.

"You've been Inland, Bates, haven't you? You've been to lots of places. If I went you'd come with me, wouldn't you?" Bates looked at her wisely and ran his beak down her arm.

"But do I want to go...? Why does Danny want me to go so far from the sea...? There'll be people there, they may speak to me. They'll look at me...what if they tried to touch me, I wouldn't know what to do. Would they be angry because I had gone to their Inland like Danny would be angry if they came to The Sands? What do you think, Bates?"

The Sands were grey and colourless that day. She stared at the open beach and at the enclosing, frowning cliffs. It was just a colourless wind-blown place. She knew every bit of it. Inland would be new and different. She had always been happy at The Sands, but now things had changed between her and Danny. Between her and The Sands. It was not the same place, not free and easy. The Sands suddenly had boundaries. Freedom was not staying here any more. Freedom was getting away.

"I'll go, Danny."

"You don't have to." He was uneasy now.

"I know. But I do really."

"Just go for a little while. Between tides. Only if you want to..."

"I'll go tomorrow."

"You have to go two hours either side of low tide. And come back in the same reach. Understand?"

"Yes."

"It's dangerous otherwise. Elder's Cave floods, that wouldn't matter to you. But Dead Man's Walk, that's dangerous. Dangerous from the sea and dangerous from the land. I don't know how you'll fare with that."

Jessie shuddered. She'd heard about Dead Man's Walk. It had come up so many times. In all Danny's stories it had been the thing that frightened her most.

"Dead Man's Walk? Where is it?"

"It's about half way."

She was ready. Danny looked at her critically for the first time, trying to see what other people would see. She was healthy, clean, she was bright, well educated ...what else...? They could not say she was not beautiful, he thought with satisfaction. But they would be critical, he knew that.

Was her skirt too long? Too short? Too uneven? He wished he knew, wished he had some shoes for her and a white pinafore...stockings? It was too late to worry, the tide was just right.

"Come on then."

"Are you coming with me?"

"Some of the way. Here, take this half sovereign. If you go to a shop you can buy something."

"How...how will I do that?" she said, taking it nervously.

"We used to play shops. It's just like that. You go in—be polite, say Good Day and please may I have one of those...or some of these..."

"What if they say I can't have them?"

"Shopkeepers are there to sell things. They'll help you. Then you give them the money and you'll get lots of change. You'll be all right Jessie, you'll get used to it." She smiled and nodded her head, rather too fast.

"You don't have to go."

"I'm going!"

He took her to Elder's Cave and they climbed the rope-ladder.

"It's dark!"

"Not completely. Your eyes will get used to it. I'll leave the lantern here for when you come back. It's a long way, just go slowly." They climbed and crawled and slithered in silence for twenty minutes and then the tunnel plunged down steeply. "Are we under the sea?"

"Yes."

"Why doesn't the sea come in then?"

73

"It never has, it's too well built. If it hadn't been this deep it would have been washed away with the cliff."

"We're going up now. It's very steep."

"You're lucky you're not carrying a pair of barrels round your shoulders," said Danny grimly. "We're inside the Misterne cliffs, we'll come to the old break soon."

"Dead Man's Walk...there it is!" said Jessie, looking ahead with horror.

The craggy path hung onto a hollow in the rock, turning and lurching with the rock face. A shelf, no more. Above, the savage cliff sheered and butted into a ceiling of rock. Far, far below the angry sea thrashed and pounded.

"It's worse in the dark," said Danny cheerfully. "You can do it, Jessie. Keep close to the cliff face...don't look down. Just follow me."

They edged slowly onto Dead Man's Walk. It was only a few yards, but it seemed like miles to Jessie before she stepped onto the rocky platform at the far end where Danny watched her last steps admiringly.

"Wasn't so bad, was it? The rest is easy, it's much wider. You'll come out under a boulder, it's probably covered with grass and bushes. Then you just have a little climb and you'll be in a big field. You'll see Misterne in the distance, walk across the field and you'll come to the road. All right?"

"Come with me, Danny."

"No. This is your adventure. You wanted to go."

"I think I want to come back now, I've had enough adventure."

They sat quietly for a moment. The silent tunnel lay ahead, the pounding sea of Dead Man's Walk behind. Suddenly Bates appeared, circling above the boiling sea and swooped to join them on the rock. Jessie laughed. "He lost us! He wouldn't come through Elder's Cave, he was afraid, weren't you Bates!" Bates glared ferociously at Danny, trying to manipulate himself closer to Jessie. She stroked his breast feathers, his wings settled and relaxed.

"He won't go through the tunnel," said Danny, getting up.

Jessie held him up and pointed him towards the mainland. "We're going that way," she said firmly. "Don't get lost again. I'm going now, Danny."

"Be sure to come back in the same reach of the tide."

"Yes. I will."

"...And if you talk to anyone...don't tell them where you come from. Where you live."

"No."

"Or how you came."

"No, I never will."

# Eleven

The grass was greener and springier Inland, that was the first thing Jessie noticed. And it didn't grow in coarse salty tufts but spread away for ever as if it was all in one piece. Danny had not told her there would be so much greenness. Bates had soon found her when she emerged cautiously from the tunnel. He had been waiting, hanging in the sky.

"Let's sit and look at it all, Bates, isn't it strange?" Bates put his head on one side. He had been here before, many times.

Jessie ate some grass—it had a nice fresh taste—and gazed around. Hedges, walls, a gate...trees! "Look at the trees, Bates," she said, "they're so big! And all different shapes. They're not like trees in books ...some of them have leaves and some of them don't..." She turned her attention to the village. It looked tiny: little houses, joined together tripping down the hill towards the sea, the harbour, its arms reaching out to sea, masts ducking and bobbing, boats closer in lying on their sides waiting for the tide. Higher up she could see the top of a church, houses set into the hill as big as a princess's palace. No people, where were the people?

"Come, Bates! It's going to be all right. I'm not afraid any more."

She ran joyfully across the field, the grass soft to her feet. She reached the wall, which was roughly made of flat stones. She could just see over the top. There was another wall just a few yards away and between the walls...the road. If she waited, perhaps something would come by, a cart, a carriage, a horse!

There was a noise coming along the road now, she ducked down behind the wall in alarm. Several noises. A soft thudding, a thwack and a shout, a moaning sort of noise. Her nose twitched, there was the most extra-ordinary smell, not unpleasant, but strange, warm. Whatever it was was going past, she could hear breathing. She stood up suddenly and looked over the wall. The road was filled with animals, dozens of brown and white backs ambling by and jostling each other. One of them stopped and reared its head, big liquid eyes stared straight at Jessie, a fat wet nose, horns...it moved on. Jessie was shaking, she couldn't move...they were all doing it now, stopping, looking at her curiously. One had a trail of green stuff hanging from its mouth, and chewed in slow, untroubled circles, the eyes were kindly, friendly.

"You're a cow," said Jessie and then she laughed and breathed freely again. "You're all cows, you've got lovely eyes and dirty bottoms. Why didn't I know!" She had seen pictures of cows before. They were four-legged animals, dotted around fields, lots of them. Not one-at-a-time animals, pushing their heads over walls. Not a road full of backs. She climbed excitedly onto the wall and looked down on them. She reached out and touched a passing back. Her hand smelt of the cow, there were some gingery hairs on it. They went on and on, a whole shoal of them, Jessie thought, warm and soft. Then they started to thin out and she could see a wriggly black and white dog barking and snapping at their heels.

"Come to me, dog," said Jessie. "Let me touch you!" The dog put its feet up on the wall and then gave a low growl and looked back down the road. There was someone there. A man. A man with breeches and boots and a smock like Danny. But not a bit like Danny. He had no beard, he was skinny and he wore a hat and carried a stick. Maybe he was a boy, how could she tell? Everything was happening very suddenly. Would he stop, would he speak?

He whistled to the dog and then he saw Jessie and slowed down.

"Morning," he grunted, and looked at her curiously. Jessie stared back, too flustered to speak. He had stopped right next to her.

"Nice day," he said. Jessie gave him a quick smile and glanced at the sea. It wasn't a nice day, there was a brisk wind blowing up out at sea, the waves would be pitching soon.

"The wind's veering..." she said hesitantly. Her voice sounded strange and unreal. Why did he stare at her so?

"You're new here, ain't you?"

"New. I don't... I'm nine..."

"I wasn't asking..." He stopped and took a couple

of steps backwards. He didn't look so friendly now. "Where have you come from?" His voice had changed, Jessie felt edgy. Why had he asked that? Danny had said...don't tell them...

"Nowhere," she said quickly, and then, "Just somewhere...somewhere far away."

The man was about to say something else but Bates suddenly plummeted from the sky, stopped himself, hovered. Jessie automatically stuck out her elbow for him to land. He did it with a lot of fuss and flapping and then glared at the man with evil pin-point eyes.

"Best be getting along then," said the man and he nearly ran after the cows. Jessie watched him go. He kept stopping and looking back. "Isn't he funny, Bates," said Jessie. "Do you think they're all like that?"

Jessie jumped down into the road and started walking towards Misterne, noticing how different everything was from The Sands. The air was softer, everything smelt different. It was strange not hearing the sea. Hearing silence instead, and the birds who sang much sweeter than sea birds though she didn't tell Bates that. The cows had been an adventure, Danny would laugh when she told him she had been afraid of them. It would be nice to have a cow she thought. Surprise Danny! Look what I've brought you from Inland! No, not a cow, there was the problem of Dead Man's Walk...A dog then, Danny would like a dog. There was so much to tell him already. The wall had ended now and she was going through a copse; she ran delightedly through the trees calling to Bates to follow.

"Bates? Where are you...Bates?" Suddenly she felt

frightened and the trees were not fun any more, they were like menacing giants looming above her and Bates was not there. She ran back with panic rising like a tidal wave and burst onto the road just as the carrier's cart trotted briskly round a corner. The carrier swerved and stopped. He waved his whip angrily.

"Silly girl! You could have had me over!"

Jessie just stood in the road, getting her breath back, staring wildly. The man stared back.

"Something wrong, is there? What's the matter? Cat got your tongue?"

"Please...I don't know..."

"Please you don't know?"

Jessie just smiled and shrugged. Perhaps she had run away, she wasn't dressed for the weather, someone was probably looking for her.

"Get in the cart," he said kindly, "I'll take you to the village."

Going in a cart! That would be something to tell Danny. She walked round it curiously.

"A horse and cart!" she said wonderingly. "Your horse has got silver feet!"

"Where have you come from?" the carrier said, thinking she was decidedly simple.

"Oh...somewhere else," Jessie said vaguely, still examining every part of the cart with interest.

"I've got to get on. Are you coming?"

"No," said Jessie suddenly, knowing she didn't want to be so close to a stranger. She needed time to get to the village, it wasn't something that could be rushed at. The carrier shrugged and twitched the reins. He would tell the postmistress about her. She would know who she was. Bates was wheeling overhead, he suddenly dived towards the road.

"Look out!" shouted the carrier. "That gull..." Bates landed on the road beside Jessie.

"It's all right," she said cheerfully. "He's mine."

Jessie skipped along the road, feeling excited now that she had got away from the trees and could see the sea again. Misterne was bigger now, she could see people moving about, pick out individual houses. The biggest houses—quality houses, the villagers called them— were on the upper slopes of Misterne. Jessie came to the driveway leading to the first one. She walked up the driveway, the house was big and square. Jessie noticed the shiny windows, the smoke coming out of an orange chimney pot, the green shutters were just like the houses in her fairy-tale book. The garden was a surprise. It was all bright, brilliant yellow. Yellow forsythia against the wall, yellow crocuses and best of all, the yellow daffodils.

"Look, Bates," she said, picking one and holding it up. "Just look! Look at the long stem, look at the shape, like...like...I don't know, like it had been cut out of paper." She started picking them and had quite a big bunch before a voice bellowed out from the house, making her jump.

"What the devil are you doing trampling about on my flower beds! Picking the flowers...you're trespassing, young lady...I've a good mind to..."

"Good day," said Jessie smiling politely. "They're

beautiful, what do you call them?" The man stared at her, startled. He was very fat and creased and had no hair. Jessie thought he must be a hundred years old.

"You're angry, aren't you?" Jessie said pleasantly.

"Angry? Angry! The nerve of the child! I'm angry all right. You walk into my garden unbidden, trample the flower beds, pick my best daffodils and then wonder that I'm angry!"

"Then you are."

"Do you usually walk into people's gardens like this?"

"No," said Jessie truthfully. She looked at the flowers in her arms. "These are yours, then?"

"Mine, of course they're mine." He was getting red in the face and flustered. He came closer to her, looked her up and down.

"Are you a gypsy? Well? Where are the rest of you? Where do you..."

"I'm going to Misterne," said Jessie suddenly. "I'm going now. Here are your flowers. I don't want them any more." She held them out, but as the man reached for them Bates fell from the sky like a stone and landed on his shiny head, flapping his wings. The man struggled and swore and tried to beat him off.

"Stop that, Bates," said Jessie calmly. "Come along, we're going now." Bates obeyed her at once and she said "Good day" and walked down the driveway. The man was speechless. He stood looking after her. When he regained his composure he sent his garden boy down to the police house.

"That was naughty, Bates," said Jessie affectionately. It had been funny watching the man fighting Bates. She was glad she had him with her.

The tide had turned. It was creeping slowly back into Elder's Cave, lifting Danny's boats. In her room a shell fell off a shelf, breaking the silence of the kilns, and making Danny jump. The silence of Jessie not being there was huge and echoing. Jessie wasn't there, she wasn't there after nine years.

She had been gone two hours.

In Misterne the shop and the post office were open. The fishermen were milling on the jetty waiting for the tide. There were children about, running errands, playing games. Jessie was not in the village yet, but the village knew she was coming, windows and doors were closing, people were talking in hushed voices.

The carrier's cart had been unloaded. The driver was sipping a cup of tea with the postmistress. Two women were whispering in a corner.

"...a little girl, just dashed out in front of him, on the corner before Breaker's Cliff... simple, he said, frightened."

"Why didn't he bring her?"

"She wouldn't come. She didn't seem to understand what he said."

"What did she look like?"

"Peculiar, long hair, thin... just a skimpy dress ...maybe a nightgown he thought."

"Must have run away..."

"I'm not so sure. She had... a seagull with her!"

"Shh! It isn't anyone from round here."

"No."

"Tom, you're making it up. What would a half-dressed slip of a girl be doing up there at this time of day?"

"I don't know, do I? She was there, Gran, watching the cows like she never seen any before. Give us a cup of tea, I'm all of a shake."

"You been spending too much time down the Smugglers'..."

"It's just eight o'clock in the morning, Gran. I tell you she was there, and she give me this real haunted feeling. I said where are you from, and she said ...'Nowhere...somewhere far away'. Gran, where's she from?"

"She's from your imagination, Tom. Don't you go talking about her round the village. They'll think you're going funny in the head like Max."

# Twelve

Jessie sniffed the air. It had changed, there was salt on it now. She had come through the farming part of Misterne without meeting anyone else on the road and she felt much more at home amongst the fishermen's cottages. There was a row of stone cottages ahead of her, a sandy space in front of them piled with nets and lobster pots. She looked in the windows but it was difficult to see clearly. The last house had an anchor propping the door open. Jessie walked in and gazed round the small room. It was so full of unknown things that it was like a treasure cave. She had to pick things up and touch them to see if they were real: painted jars, dried flowers, strange glass shapes, little framed pictures and mirrors.

Jessie pushed open a door that led into the kitchen. There was a fire burning, an old woman sitting beside it baiting hooks. Her head was bowed, she had thin white hair, Jessie could see her pink head underneath it. Her stiff fingers fumbled with the hooks.

"I'll help you," said Jessie, going and kneeling beside her. The old woman's head wavered, she grunted and stabbed viciously at a hook, missing it.

"Let me do them all," said Jessie. "You'll hurt yourself."

The old woman sat very still, then she put out her hand, groping, as if she was trying to find Jessie and couldn't.

"You're not... You're not Jenny's girl," she said in a quavery voice. "Who are you?" Jessie looked up at her face and dropped the hooks. She stifled a little scream. Pale unmoving eyes stared from deep sockets. There was no life in them, nothing.

She remembered the dunlin, its eyes savagely pecked. Danny saying "No, Jessie, you can't keep it. It can't see, don't you understand?"

"You can't see!" Jessie said, shocked and frightened that it could happen to a person too. She reached out with terrible pity to touch the woman's face. The old woman caught her hand in a grip like a talon. "Let me go. Please, don't do that. I don't like it." The old woman shook her head from side to side.

"I know who you are."

"You don't. You can't know."

"You shouldn't have come here."

"Why not? Why not?"

"Go back. Go back where you came from. You won't be welcome here." Her hand went slack and dropped to her lap. Jessie stumbled into the other room and out of the door as someone came in the back way.

"Mother? What's going on here? Mother, are you all right?"

The old lady was shaking. "Poor little thing. She shouldn't have come."

"Who? Mother, who? Has someone been here?"

Jessie stumbled out of the house and started to run towards the sea. The little cobbled streets ran into each other and branched away again in a confusion of lines. People standing outside their houses went in and closed the doors when they saw her coming. Curtains twitched, Jessie felt eyes watching, following her. She reached the beach next to the jetty. There was no one there, she sat down and watched the fishing boats putting out to sea. She didn't want to meet anyone else, not for a while anyway. She felt sad for the old lady, and sorry now that she had been afraid of her blindness. It had been so unexpected. Meeting people wasn't easy. It was quite hard. They were all different.

Bates flew out to sea with the fishing boats. A stripy cat was making its way towards Jessie. It sniffed at a fish head, investigated a hunk of seaweed and chased a piece of paper that fluttered in the wind. Jessie was intrigued, the cat made her laugh. There had been cats on The Sands once, Danny had told her about them waiting for the fish to be unloaded, told her of their cunning. He would like a cat, she knew he would. Much better than a dog. Yes...a cat for Danny...

The little post office was crowded with women. They had stopped pretending that they had come to buy a stamp or send a letter. They locked the door and got to grips with serious gossip and speculation. Miss Potter had to rap sharply at the door to get in. She stood quietly, listening to the rising panic with impatience and disapproval.

"Should we get the parson to come? He'd know

what to do with a spirit."

"If the parson comes...well, we're as good as admitting we believe in ghosts, aren't we?"

"We have to, don't we? When people have *seen* her!"

"Have they though, really?"

"Tom's seen her."

"Tom's seen things before."

"He *spoke* to her! So did the carrier. She's from out there. She's got to be and we all know what *that* means!"

Miss Potter twitched nervously. Such ridiculous talk, such ignorant women. It would unsettle the children when they came back to school the next day.

"What *does* it mean?" she said in her rather grand voice.

"Seeing someone from...from out there...it's a bad omen..."

"There'll be some tragedy, you'll see, Miss Potter. It's a dire warning for us all."

"Stuff and nonsense! You're being very childish and superstitious." The women stared at her with contempt.

"You wouldn't understand, Miss Potter. You haven't been here long enough. We know."

"It's a spirit girl. She probably wouldn't show herself to you."

"A girl?" said Miss Potter twitching again, thinking of Lisa. "Surely you can't all be frightened of an imaginary girl! Do be reasonable. Has anyone really seen this...this..."

"*Girl.* She looked in my window and ran away."

"And what did she look like exactly?"

"I couldn't say *exactly*. Spirit folk aren't exact by nature. She was...wispy...small, waif-like..."

"She was wearing grey swirly things, wasn't she, Grace. Like something from a grave..."

"And there was a bird with her. A big gull. The whole house went cold, like something passing over ...and don't say I imagined it, Miss Potter. I know what happened."

"But no one has really seen her, not close up," said Miss Potter.

"Old Rose did."

"Yes! Rose did!"

"Old Rose," said Miss Potter triumphantly, "is blind!"

"Rose knew. She's old enough to remember. She used to live out there. She knew by the smell."

"You're telling me this imaginary child...smells too?"

"Yes. Sort of damp, like an old sea cave. Rose knew where she came from all right." They all nodded then and turned away from her. Miss Potter started rummaging for her smelling salts, she was feeling faint. There was a knock on the door and everyone swung round fearfully.

"It's just my Davey," said the postmistress, "back from his errands." She let him in and, after looking cautiously up and down the street, she left the door open.

"Why were you all locked in?" asked Davey, looking at the frightened faces. "I came to tell you...you seem to know already."

"Know what?"

"There's a ghost running round the village. A real one!" His eyes shone with excitement. "It's a girl from The Sands!" Several people clutched at each other in fear. Miss Potter took a big sniff at her smelling salts.

The news about Jessie gradually sifted through the farmland and Morgan took it back to Lisa. He was stunned by her reaction.

"A girl...my age...everyone turning her away and saying..."

"Calm down, Lisa. Hey! Where are you going?"

"It's Jessie!" she said, throwing her shawl across her shoulders. "It's Jessie! Jessie's come!"

"Lisa, come back..." She didn't hear him, she was off and running like the wind down to the village.

It seemed deserted. Shutters were closed, there wasn't even a dog about. She saw Davey streak by and hammer on the post office door. She followed him. Everyone was looking at Davey, Lisa pushed herself into the crowd.

"Did you see anything, love?" his mother asked earnestly.

"No. But the carrier did. He's at the police station. And she appeared out of nowhere and scared Tom and his cows. Chased them down the road...wailing and that. He was really scared. And she went into Mr Carrington's house and ripped up his flowers, and she's got this seagull tried to tear Mr Carrington's eyes out. Mr Carrington's garden boy said it was really frightening, like something evil had come..."

90

"You're lying! It's not true, she's not evil..." Lisa could control herself no longer, she ran back to the door. Several people tried to stop her but she struggled like a wildcat and got away from them.

"Bring her back!" called Miss Potter weakly. But no one would go after her.

# Thirteen

The cat was moving closer to Jessie. "Come cat," she said quietly. "Come here, come back with me." The cat came to her and rubbed its head against her arm. She sat very still. It started to make a rumbling noise and Jessie decided it was being friendly. She reached out her hand and touched it, stroked it, and then she pulled it on to her knee and held it close to her, feeling its warmth and a sudden rush of love and gratitude. "Come and be Danny's cat," she whispered. "Please do that, will you?"

She held it a little away from her to look into its eyes. Suddenly Bates was back, he swooped round Jessie screeching fiercely. The cat dug its claws into Jessie's shoulder and bounded away. Bates came and nibbled her finger.

"It's no good being nice now," she said crossly, but she soon relented and stroked his head. "Maybe the cat belongs to someone, like the flowers. Maybe it wouldn't have wanted to come."

Now she had nothing to take back to Danny. There was a small fisherman's shop on the quay, it sold hooks and lines and rods, tobacco and pipes. Jessie had noticed it earlier, and tried to pretend it wasn't there. But there was still time to wait for the tide to drop, time before she had to make her way up the cliff again. She felt the coin knotted in her sash. "Come on, Bates," she said at last. "We're going shopping!"

She fiddled helplessly with the latch until a woman came and opened the door.

"It's not locked," she said, looking critically at Jessie. "You just had to lift the latch."

"Yes. Thank you," said Jessie.

The woman was suddenly battling with the door. "Get out! Go on, shoo! Greedy gulls," she said to Jessie, "they get in everywhere."

"It's all right, he's with me," said Jessie.

"Oh yes? Well, he can wait outside. You take him everywhere, do you?"

"Yes. I mean...he just comes." She was fumbling nervously with her money and looking for something she could buy. It wasn't the way she'd played shops with Danny...one fish for seventeen shells, twenty pebbles for five yards of rope...

"I haven't seen you here before, have I?" asked the woman. "Have you come in a boat?"

"Yes," said Jessie, and then knowing it was a lie, "No...not really..."

The woman was looking at her suspiciously now. Jessie was getting used to the look.

"Are you going to buy something? What is it you want?"

"I don't know," said Jessie helplessly, and she turned suddenly, fumbled with the latch on the door and ran away, leaving it swinging open.

The woman watched her climbing over the sea wall

93

and going towards the cliffs with her seagull. She thought she would just go up to the post office ...perhaps someone there would know about the strange girl. She sniffed and glanced around her. The shop smelt damp, seaweedy.

Lisa came skidding down the harbour road and rushed into the shop.

"Have you seen a girl..." she panted.

"Yes. Weird, who is she? I've never seen..."

"Which way did she go?"

"Over towards the cliffs. Lisa, don't go after her. Lisa! Don't go. *She isn't one of us!*"

Jessie had had enough of Misterne. People were not what she had expected at all. They weren't a bit like Danny. They were cold and hostile, the old blind woman had been right saying she wouldn't be welcome! She thought she could work her way round the cliff without having to go near the village again.

"Jessie! Jessie, wait...please wait for me!" Jessie glanced back and saw a girl stumbling after her and waving. She quickened her pace, several minutes later she came to an outcrop of rocks and blackthorn. She stopped and looked back. The girl was still coming, she was alone. She knew Jessie's name.

"Jessie!" Lisa came puffing out of breath towards her and stopped. "Please don't run away. I want to be your friend. Please?"

Jessie stared down at her, tense, poised to run. Lisa knew she had to be careful, speak quietly, move slowly. It was like approaching a wild animal, she

94

even had a look of the wild about her. But it was Jessie, Jessie here, Jessie real. Lisa went on smiling, absorbing everything she could about Jessie. Her deep blue restless eyes, her long fair hair falling round her shoulders like a waterfall. Her thin arms, her bare dirty feet. She must be cold, she had on the skimpiest summer dress that blew in the wind, she wore no petticoats, not even a bodice underneath. She should have looked like a beggar's child, but there was an elegance about her that was so striking she didn't even look poor.

Lisa sat down and patted the grass beside her. "Come and talk to me, Jessie. Come and sit with me."

Jessie didn't move. She was trapped. There was still time to wait before the tide would be low enough to go back. But this girl would see where she went, she might follow her... The girl was friendly enough, she smiled continually out of her freckled face. Jessie was intrigued to see how her hair curled like the Irish Moss seaweed, and her black legs and trimly booted feet peeped out from layers of heavy clothes covered by a shawl that seemed to be made of fuzzy thick lace.

"I'm Lisa...I live on a farm at the top of Misterne, it's right up there, with my father. We have a pig and some chickens and...and..." She waited but Jessie did not speak. "I always hoped you'd come one day. You're from The Sands, aren't you? It's all right, I won't tell anyone. You don't want me to, do you?"

Jessie moved a step closer to Lisa but she didn't speak, she just looked.

"Do say something! Jessie? You've never been

anywhere before, have you...have you? Met anyone
...except your father...Danny, isn't it? Don't worry, I
won't tell anyone...Oh Jessie, it must be
strange...I'd be frightened if it was me, not knowing
what it would be like coming here and..."

Bates suddenly swooped low over Lisa's head, making her flinch. He landed and settled on a rock over
Jessie's head and nuzzled her hair with his beak.

"He's tame!" said Lisa delightedly. "Is he yours?
Can I touch him?"

"No! He won't let you, he's mine."

"Very well, I won't. What's his name?"

"Bates."

"Oh...nice...does he go everywhere with you?"

"Yes."

"Oh. If you're staying long...you could come to the
farm and see our chickens? Are you going to stay?
Well...will you come back again?"

"No. I don't like it here. I don't like the way people
look at me."

"Oh Jessie..."

"They don't want me here, I know they don't."

"I do."

"Yes. I don't know why. You're different."

"Do let's be friends, come and sit near me...People
are frightened of you because...because they don't
think anyone's lived on The Sands for ages and ages."

"But you knew..." said Jessie slowly, "you're not
frightened."

"Not a bit." Jessie moved towards her, she sat down
a little distance away and Bates settled next to her.

"Frightened of me!" Jessie said and gave a little laugh. Lisa laughed too.

"If you came back to the village with me it would be all right, then they'd see you were just ordinary. Will you?"

"Maybe. Not today."

"I have to go to school tomorrow. We've got a day off while the roof's mended. Come back tomorrow and come to school with me...you've never been to school, have you?"

"Danny's got lots of books. What's school like?"

"It's...it's fine," lied Lisa. "You'd like it. And it would be easier...just having to meet boys and girls, wouldn't it? Until they got used to you."

"Yes," said Jessie, thinking about it.

"Then you could make lots of friends. Isn't it lonely out there?"

"Danny's there," she said, thinking about him, wondering how she would get away from Lisa. She had to, the tide was falling rapidly.

"Will you go away now? Please, Lisa?" Lisa felt slapped in the face.

"But we're just getting to be friends..."

"I've had enough of being friends."

"Oh *Jessie!*"

"I want to go back."

"How do you get there?"

"You're not to know."

"I'll see where you go, won't I? Jessie, I won't tell anyone."

"No, no! Go away!"

"You can trust me, Jessie! I will go, I won't watch where you go. But come back tomorrow, I'll see you here. Jessie?"

"Maybe. At low tide...maybe..."

It was much worse going back across Dead Man's Walk without Danny saying "Don't look down". She did look down and the sea was really angry. She had never been afraid of the sea before, it was being so far above it, looking down, defying it that made it seem like an enemy that would reach out and grab her. If there was a Sea Monster that didn't belong to a story, then it would live down there.

Danny had done everything: brought firewood, made the fire, fetched water from the stream, collected seaweed, swept the house.

Jessie looked round uneasily. "Why Danny, why? Did you think I wasn't coming back? Did you?" He was kind and pleased to see her, but he was distant, too. Her adventures Inland seemed dull and timid now. Danny went out in the boat that night, not to go anywhere, just to get away. He knew she was unhappy, knew that Inland had thrown her back. But she would go again. He couldn't help her, he had to push her away from him, he had to start to break the bond.

There had been a disturbance out at sea that afternoon just before Jessie came back. He had seen it start over the village, unnatural wave formations that went against the wind, then a sudden calm. He had seen it once before and his heart sank like a stone. Mara was close. He had thought that when the time came he would be able to take it. He had never known it would be so hard to part with Jessie.

Jessie cried herself to sleep waiting for Danny to come back. She didn't belong anywhere. Certainly not in Misterne, and now not even on The Sands, not even with Danny. She felt she was being torn in two pieces and nothing would ever put her together again. When Danny came back she was having a nightmare about the Sea Monster. It was waiting for her in the foam underneath Dead Man's Walk. It wanted to seize her and take her away and she was frightened because she wanted to go.

She was calling out for her mother. She had always called for Danny before.

# Fourteen

Lisa was waiting in the same place on the cliff.

"I didn't know if you'd be here," said Jessie, relieved.

Lisa was delighted that Jessie had come, and that she seemed pleased to see her. She had been waiting and hoping that Jessie would come.

"Where's Bates?"

"Fishing. He'll come soon. Are we going to school?"

"Yes... if you want to. But it's not for ages yet. Let's go and walk on the cliff. I've got a special cave, no one knows where it is. You can hide in it if you want to."

Jessie looked at her in surprise.

"Hide? I don't need to hide... you mean from... you've told them, haven't you, they're not frightened any more?"

"Well, yes, but..."

"What's wrong then? You said they thought I couldn't be here because no one lived on The Sands any more. But I am here. I'm here again, aren't I?" Jessie sat down suddenly and defiantly and glared at Lisa.

"Don't be angry with me, it's not my fault," said Lisa. "I just want to be your friend."

"Why you? Why not other people?"

"I believe in you, they don't yet. Oh, it's so silly but...do you know what a ghost is, Jessie?"

"Ghost?" Jessie looked startled. "Danny says The Sands are full of the ghosts of old smugglers. He used to try and scare me with them sometimes. But I wasn't scared, I think ghosts are fun. Danny's are anyway." Jessie's expression changed suddenly. "Do they think I'm a ghost? Is that what you've been trying to say?"

Lisa nodded, embarrassed, and Jessie started to laugh a gentle, infectious laugh. Lisa was taken aback to start with, but as she watched Jessie she caught the simple craziness of the situation and began to laugh too.

"Danny says ghosts can walk through walls and they drag clanking chains and go *Whooo-oooooo!*"

"Yes! And they carry their heads under their arms and go *Aaaaaarghh!*"

"They come out of graves...and they don't leave footprints!" Jessie ran off suddenly towards the cliff.

"Where are you going?"

"Bates is looking for me."

Lisa waited for her to come back, thinking how different she was from anyone else, with her suddenly changing moods. She hoped she wouldn't change her mind about going to school. It was going to cause a sensation, she could imagine it already. Miss Potter's moustache would dance right off her face when she saw that Jessie was real. The others would be wild with envy when they saw that she was Lisa's special friend. Lisa! The only one who could get through to the mystery girl! Some of Jessie's mystery would rub off on her. The other girls would let her join their games now, share their secrets.

Jessie came back with Bates. "So everything's all right now. You've told them I'm not a ghost."

"Yes," said Lisa truthfully. She had tried to but no one had listened. They had said she was making it all up, or that she was in touch with bad spirits. Some of them had even crossed the street when she went by, rather than risk touching her. It had been a bit eerie and even her father had not really believed her—or wanted to. Only Max would have truly believed and the old man had been taken to the Infirmary in the town the day before with chest pains.

Lisa stood up. "Shall we go now?"

"Yes," said Jessie uncertainly, looking at Lisa. She had a blue dress on today and a white pinafore and carried her slate. "Does everyone dress like you?"

"Most do. Don't you...feel cold, Jessie? Don't you wear shoes and stockings?"

"No. I've got some shoes for the winter. Danny made them. It doesn't matter, does it, what you wear?"

Lisa tried to imagine what Miss Potter would say when she saw Jessie's clothes. "It doesn't matter the first day," she said cheerfully.

Lisa led Jessie over the hill to the side of Misterne, away from the village. It would take much longer. She didn't want to walk through the village. She was afraid of what people might do to Jessie.

"Lisa...is the school big?"

"No. It's a part of the Squire's barn. He gave it to

the village to start a school. It's cold. The roof fell in last week but they've put it up again now. Miss Potter teaches us, she's a bit strict but don't worry, I'll ask her if you can sit with me." She felt possessive about Jessie suddenly and hoped she wouldn't make lots of friends. Not at first anyway. Jessie belonged to her.

"Come on, we're nearly there."

"Wait," said Jessie, hanging back. "How did you know my name? Were you expecting me to come?"

"Max told me about you...Max! Of course, you must have heard of him, he used to live at The Sands, he knew your father and your grandfather!"

"Max? Yes, Danny told me about Max," said Jessie slowly. "Do you see him...talk to him...just like you do to me?"

"Well of course...what's wrong, Jessie?"

What's wrong? Jessie thought that there must be something strangely wrong with Lisa. Max had been washed out to sea in the big storm, just after she was born. Danny had built a cairn of stones in his memory, so Lisa couldn't have met Max...

"Come *on*, Jessie, we're there. You can hold my hand if you like."

"Why?" said Jessie, edging away.

Miss Potter had just settled the children down to their first lessons. The older ones worked at one end and the little ones at the other. She had her desk by a wall and there was a rusty stove in the middle. She had marked the register and noted with some dismay that Lisa was absent. The other children had come in agog with rumours about the strange girl and she had told them very firmly that the strange girl did not exist and anyone else mentioning anything about the silly rumours would be punished. Then the door swung open. Bates flew in and swooped up to a rafter above her head. Lisa and Jessie were framed in the door.

"Lisa!"

"Sorry I'm late, Miss Potter. This is Jessie."

The shocked silence was a solid thing, it held for a moment and then it was shattered. Chair legs rasped on the boards, some fell over as the children panicked and ran for doors and windows. There were gasps, whimpers, little screams and then one voice above the rest...

"It's her! From The Sands! Don't let her come in, she isn't one of us!"


It was some time before Miss Potter had calmed the school and settled them all up at one end of the barn in charge of the bigger girls. She managed not to look at Jessie who was sitting with Lisa in the dunce's corner, shielded by a store cupboard.

She took some deep breaths to calm herself. The wretched child didn't exist, but she was here and the only thing she could do...well, she couldn't ignore her when...she couldn't play pretend games, she was the schoolmistress...

She picked up her register and walked as bravely as she could to the girls in the corner. There were two of them. Definitely two. And the seagull had flown down and made a mess on the table. It glared at her evilly.

"Now then...Lisa, get rid of that bird at once."

"I can't, Miss Potter. It's Jessie's. He's called Bates, he goes everywhere with her."

"Don't be impertinent, Lisa. Stop smirking."

Jessie looked at them both and then at Bates. "Go, Bates," she said, pointing up to the rafters. "Up there." Bates gave a final glare at Miss Potter and went and perched on the rafter, looking down protectively at Jessie.

"Yes...well now," said Miss Potter, fiddling with her register.

"Jessie's come to school," said Lisa brightly.

"Doesn't she know she should stand with her hands folded when an elder speaks to her?" Lisa opened her mouth and shut it again quickly. She was about to say that Miss Potter hadn't spoken to Jessie. She hadn't even looked at her yet.

"Get two chairs and sit down," said Miss Potter quickly. Jessie sat directly opposite her, with supreme effort Miss Potter raised her eyes. She saw a child, strangely dressed, with a half-wild look and piercing blue eyes. But a child who looked anxious and ill at ease.

"What's your name?" she asked quietly.

"Jessie. I can come to school, can't I?"

"We'll have to see, won't we."

"But I am here. When do we do the lessons?"

"In good time. Have you been to school before?"

"No, but I've done lessons..."

"The first thing you have to learn is that schools have rules. We'll have to teach you some manners, I can see. We do not bring birds to school. At lunch-time you will...take it away. Supposing all the pupils brought pets to school?"

"Yes," said Jessie and turned to Lisa. "What would you bring? One of your chickens? Or would you..."

"Enough!" said Miss Potter crossly and opened her register at a new page. "Now...I'm sure you can come to school Je...Jessie...But I should speak to your parents...and...er...Just give me the details now. What's your name?"

"Jessie," said Jessie, giving Lisa a puzzled look.

"You have another name?"

"Do you, Jessie?" said Lisa. "I never thought ...does Danny..."

"Lisa! Quiet!"

"That name," said Jessie, "Bates."

"Bates! So that's why..."

"Lisa, you'll have to go..."

"No, please, don't send Lisa away!" Miss Potter glared at them both. She didn't want to send Lisa away and be left alone with the child.

"Address? Where do you live?"

"The Sands," said Jessie firmly. It was no secret any more.

Miss Potter's pen stuck in the paper and made a big blot.

"Does your house have a name?"

"No," said Jessie, laughing lightly. "Does yours?"

"Most houses have a name or a number..."

"We live in the kilns, it's the only house there."

Miss Potter wrote The Kilns. She couldn't bring

herself to write The Sands. "Fine. And how old are you?"

"Nine."

"Nine. And do you know your birth date?"

"Of course. The first quarter of the moon before the spring equinox."

"That's March..." interrupted Lisa.

"Yes," said Jessie patiently. "Last week I had my birthday and Danny..."

"Just answer the questions," said Miss Potter.

"Why are there so many questions? I just want to come to school!"

"There are...formalities," said Miss Potter severely. "You can't just come."

"But I *have* come. I'm here!" she said desperately. "Aren't I?"

Miss Potter pushed the register away. The child was getting upset, she might become uncontrollable. The other children were restive. She found a simple reading book. "Do you know your letters?" Jessie looked at it puzzled—A is an Apple. B is for Baby—"Letters? I had one of those books before I could read."

"You read?" Miss Potter said with a little disbelieving laugh. "Perhaps you'd care to read to me from my Bible?"

"If you like," said Jessie. "I'll read about David and Goliath. Danny likes that. It's all right, thank you, I know where to find it."

Miss Potter tried to hide her astonishment as Jessie read fluently. Lisa gaped at her friend in awe. It was the same when Miss Potter gave Jessie some sums and she did them effortlessly. "Explain how you worked them out," said Miss Potter, as if Jessie had cheated.

"Danny says it doesn't matter how you do them. If you get them right it doesn't matter how."

"Danny's your father?" Jessie nodded proudly. "And he's taught you so far? Show me your writing then. Copy this on Lisa's slate..."

"Danny says I shouldn't copy. I should always make things out of my own head."

"Oh *indeed!*" Miss Potter said, thinking grimly that "Danny says" would have to be banned if she was going to teach Jessie.

"I'll write about hermit crabs...no, I've done that...I'll write about the dream I had last night." She looked curiously at Lisa's slate. Miss Potter found her a piece of paper and pen and ink. She watched her start to write, quickly and neatly, her hair falling onto the desk like a waterfall. She had to admit that the child had been extraordinarily well educated. Like a child of the gentry, not like an ignorant Misterner. The Schools Inspector would be most impressed to see her work...amazed...and it would reflect on Miss Potter's teaching. Miss Potter suddenly pulled herself together. What could she be thinking about! She was believing in her already, seeing an everyday future ahead! Fluttering nervously, she wished some other adult would come. The responsibility was too great. But no one would. It was not even the parson's day to come and take religious instruction.

She turned back to the other children. They clustered round her, wide-eyed, whispering nervously

...Who is she? Why is she here? Send her away, ma'am, please send her away! Tom's Mum said... Jane's crying because she wet herself... I want to go home...

"Be quiet and compose yourselves," snapped Miss Potter. She made the children turn round and face away from Jessie. She tried to turn away herself and shut Jessie off. But she was there every time she looked up. She was still there, every time.

Jessie had finished writing about her dream by lunchtime. She kept glancing out of the window, smiling secretly.

"What is it, Jessie?"

"A storm, a big one, it's coming soon."

"How can you tell?"

"Can't you? It's out at sea now but it will be here soon. Shall we go out now?"

"We can't, it's not allowed. We have to have our lunch here. You haven't got anything to eat, have you? You can share mine." Lisa unwrapped her piece of bread and cheese and broke it in two. Jessie smelt it suspiciously. "What is it?"

"Cheese. I suppose you've never had cheese...or butter, or milk, have you?"

"I know about them," Jessie said. "Danny told me. He didn't say they smelt rotten though."

Miss Potter was hovering uneasily. "Jessie hasn't any lunch, ma'am. She won't share *mine*," said Lisa, looking at her teacher pointedly.

"She shall have mine," said Miss Potter quickly.

She was feeling most peculiar and incapable of eating a mouthful. The Parsonage cook had given her a slice of mutton pie that morning. She unwrapped it and pushed it towards Jessie.

"There you are, be grateful," she said. "Nice mutton pie. Eat it all up now."

"What is it?"

"Mutton, meat," said Lisa. "Danny must have told you about meat. It comes from a sheep."

Jessie poked it with her finger cautiously. Sheep, she thought, sheep, wool, woolly, warm, kind eyes like the cows' eyes... an animal like the cat on the beach... She stood up and her chair fell over with a bang that silenced the school. She was staring at Miss Potter with loathing. "You killed a sheep?"

"No, no, of course *I* didn't..."

"How did you do it? How?"

"You don't have to eat it..."

"*Eat* it! *Eat* it!" Jessie's sudden wildness had a shattering effect on Miss Potter, she was beginning to feel faint, Jessie was drifting out of focus... Please God send someone to help me. I can't cope with this child. She isn't real, she's not like the others... help me...

"Miss Potter? Miss Potter, are you ill?"

A child screamed, somewhere far away. Miss Potter reached for a chair. It wasn't there. She hit her head on a bench as she fell...

When she opened her eyes again the doctor was there and some anxiously peering parents' faces. Children were being shepherded away, there was urgent whispering, arguing, hushing. Only one thing became clear to Miss Potter.

*Jessie had gone and taken Lisa with her.*

# Fifteen

It was nearing midnight and lights were burning all over Misterne as the parson's pony trap made its way through the narrow streets. Mrs Madden pulled her cloak round her, shivering slightly. She could feel the village's fear, it hung over the houses like a haunting mist, but she said nothing to her husband about it. He had no time for local superstitions and idle talk about wandering spirits.

They had both been shocked when they returned home late from visiting an outlying village to find Miss Potter writhing in her bed, tearing at her nightgown and muttering wildly that a weird nymph-like child had come from The Sands to steal her soul. The frightened maid explained how the doctor had brought her home in this state from school. The parson grunted when she reported the gossip about Jessie, but when he heard that Lisa was missing, search parties were out and women and children had battened themselves in the Inn too terrified to go home until the menfolk returned, he harnessed the tired pony again.

Ben the landlord was glad to see the Maddens arrive. He ushered Mrs Madden into the main bar where the women and children were gathered in little wary groups, looking to her for help.

The parson joined the policeman and the doctor who were conferring in the Snug bar. "Thank you for bringing Miss Potter home," he said to the doctor, "she's sleeping now..." He shook his head and looked to them for an explanation.

"She had a nervous fit, fell and hit her head...that and shock..." said the doctor.

"Do you know what happened?"

"Two of the children came for me, they were too distraught to make sense but it was plain something serious had happened at the school. When I got there the place was in uproar, Miss Potter was lying on the floor. The children were mostly speechless with fear but I gathered that an unknown girl had turned up that morning with Lisa Morgan. They thought she was a ghost and they were badly frightened. Mass hysteria is my diagnosis, I haven't come across it before but I've heard about it. Children are very imaginative. George doesn't agree, do you, George?"

"Well sir...I wouldn't be contradicting the doctor, of course...but there were a number of reports yesterday about an unusual girl in the village. They said she'd come from The Sands, you see..."

"Surely you don't believe that," said the parson brusquely, his eyes narrowed... "Do you?"

"No, no, sir, of course I don't. There's no way to get there anyway...I mean...I think there was *someone*. Maybe a gypsy child, maybe the mad child from one of the quality houses up the hill. We wouldn't know, would we? They'd have kept her locked away, wouldn't they? The youngsters said she had a seagull with her, there were bird droppings in the school. No evidence of a child."

"And she just went away...and took little Lisa," said the parson thoughtfully. "What does Morgan say?"

The policeman looked at the doctor who looked slightly uncomfortable. "Morgan says Lisa invents pretend friends—she's a lonely child..."

"And one of them has come to life?" the parson said sarcastically.

"One of them was a girl called Jessie who lived on The Sands. Morgan's out on the cliffs now with a search party. There's a storm coming..."

"On the *cliffs*?" The parson turned to the policeman. "Why are you searching out there and not inland?"

Mrs Madden quietly organized the women and children out of their huddles and into action. She set the children off on a guessing game, and then persuaded their mothers to go into the Inn's kitchens and make some hot drinks. She tried to draw the children to speak about the morning's happenings but most of them were shy and afraid. Not Harry though. He always kept apart from the other children, a thoughtful lad who lived on a remote farm, like Lisa.

"Don't you want to play a game, Harry?"

"No, thank you, ma'am."

"A penny for your thoughts then?" said Mrs Madden, sitting next to him. He got up, embarrassed. "Sit by me, Harry, I don't bite little boys' heads off you know."

"Yes, ma'am... I mean... no, ma'am..."

"Aren't you tired?"

"No! I never been up this late, nothing's ever happened like this before!" Mrs Madden noted a little gleam of excitement in his eyes. He didn't look nervously over his shoulder as the other children did.

"Is Lisa a friend of yours, Harry?"

"She's a girl, ma'am," said Harry, looking round quickly in case he was being overheard.

"So she is!" Mrs Madden said, giving him a winky look. "So I don't suppose she ever wasted her breath talking to you!"

"She did... she... what's happened to her?"

"That's what we all want to know."

"Some say she's been kidnapped and the others say..." He stopped and frowned.

"What do the others say?"

"That they sent for her, from The Sands."

"Who did?"

"I don't know." Harry wriggled uncomfortably. "Please ma'am, I'll be in trouble, talking about it."

"Not this time, Harry, not if it helps to find Lisa safe. Did Lisa talk about The Sands to you?"

"She used to, then she stopped. She knew Jessie was there, Max told her. You could ask Max?" Harry looked hopeful.

"Max is very ill. He's in the Infirmary," said Mrs Madden. "Tell me what happened when Jessie came to school."

"She came with Lisa and everyone was frightened."

"Even you?"

Harry smiled shyly and shook his head. "Not until afterwards, when people...grown-up people said she hadn't really been there at all. Then it was frightening because I had seen her."

"What did she look like?"

"She had a seagull and it did just what she told it to do. She didn't look anything special. Poor, she didn't wear shoes...nor a pinafore or anything, just a ragged dress and she smelt peculiar."

"Oh?"

"Pardon, ma'am...like seaweed I mean, or like a sea cave. Not..."

"That's all right," said Mrs Madden quickly. "Did you speak to this Jessie?"

"No. No one did. Just Miss Potter...and Lisa, of course. May I go now, ma'am? She's gone with Jessie, wherever Jessie goes. I can't tell you any more."

Mrs Madden smiled and nodded gratefully. "We'll both pray for Lisa to come back safely, won't we, Harry?" Harry nodded but when he turned to go away she saw him give a little hopeless shrug. Mrs Madden knew what he meant, but she put it out of her mind, reminding herself that she was the parson's wife.

Morgan was tortured with his fears for Lisa, his temper was fraying. He had been angry earlier when the doctor and the policeman had interviewed him and made him feel Lisa's disappearance was his fault. They had hinted that she was a lonely child, that they'd had a row, they'd even asked about Lisa's mother, suggesting to Morgan that if she had been with her mother, or in a conventional family, none of this fuss would ever have happened. Morgan had stalked out. Now he was angry again because the search party had been called off until daylight and the men had all gone home. It was well past midnight now and the storm had broken, threatening to hurl him into the sea. He fought against the wind and spray, taking strength from the challenge.

Lisa had to be found. She had to come back, life without her would be...he thrust the thought of it away from him. The sea was pounding against the sea wall now with great thuds, he felt it shake and judder and ran doubled up towards the village road. He sheltered in the door of the fishermen's shop on the quay. There was a figure coming up from the beach. So they hadn't all run for home, Morgan thought grimly. He waited, it would be good to have a bit of company. The figure moved slowly with a shuffling, familiar gait. Morgan felt suddenly chilled. "Max!" he said, "Max! It is you, isn't it?"

He stepped out into the wind towards the figure. There was a long streak of lightning, it seemed to stop in time and hang in the sky. Max stood, eerily lit. Water streamed off him, he looked older than time and Morgan's fear gripped him anew.

"Where's Lisa?" Morgan said dangerously. *"What have you done to her?"*

Max pushed past Morgan to the shelter of the shop door and then turned round slowly. "Lisa has gone to The Sands..."

"No! She can't...she couldn't...oh God, no..."

"She'll be all right, Morgan. She'll come back after the storm, when the tide falls. She can't get back before then." Morgan stared at him wildly. The violence in him ebbed away, Max was so calm, so sure.

"How do you know? How could she get there...Max, are you sure..."

"Don't worry. She went with Jessie, but she'll have to come back alone. She will come, believe me."

"Then I can go after her..."

"No. Stay calm, ask no questions and I'll show you where to wait for her."

"Yes, Max," said Morgan, quietly humble. He gazed at the old man steadily and saw the terrible sadness in his face.

"Yes, Max. I'll do anything you say. You came from The Sands, didn't you? You're one of them. You know."

Max had left him, suddenly and silently on the cliff. Morgan sheltered behind a rock and watched the storm blow itself out and the dawn break reluctantly from the grey washed-out sky. Lisa would come soon, he knew, he had only to wait for the tide to drop a little further... Never since the world began, he could swear afterwards, had a tide taken so long to go out.

And then she was there, struggling up from the cliff, wet, frightened, alone.

"Lisa!"

She was there, suddenly, sobbing on his shoulder. "I came back alone...I had to...Jessie's gone...

across Dead Man's Walk...alone..."

"You're all right, you're not hurt...Lisa, it's over, you're safe, stop crying."

"I can't stop. Jessie's gone, she's gone forever."

"Hush, never mind now. I'll carry you back, come..."

"Danny's alone." Morgan picked her up and set out across the field as fast as he could.

"I was so frightened of Dead Man's Walk," she said faintly, "but it was easy when I got there...someone came to guide me..."

"Who?"

"I couldn't see...someone I know...like..." Her voice faltered and stopped.

"Like Max," said Morgan.

# Sixteen

Lisa could never remember those first few days in the big feather bed at the parsonage. Her father was there a lot, wiping her face and murmuring her name. The doctor's voice broke through once. "She can't hear you, Morgan," he said tersely. "It's a fever of the brain."

"Will she get better?"

"I'm doing everything possible."

"Yes, sir, I'm sorry. But when she does..."

"*If* she does...she probably won't remember anything about this silly fantasy."

She was hot and achy and she dreamed hazy dreams even when she was awake. Gradually she became aware of the people around her and knew that the big firm hands nursing her belonged to Mrs Madden and the small uncertain ones to her maid.

The policeman came when Mrs Madden thought Lisa was well enough to talk to him.

"But just for a moment," said Mrs Madden sternly, "and I shall stop you at once if the child is distressed."

The policeman was quite distressed himself. He was used to dealing with felons or thieves, but this case—a possible murder investigation, his superiors had said—was ghoulish. He wanted to believe the people who said the Morgan girl had invented the whole story to draw attention to herself. The alternative troubled him. He did not want to be with someone who walked and talked with spirits and had been to The Sands.

"This...er...alleged girl..." he said, pulling out his notebook. "How...where did you...uhm...come upon her?"

"Tell the policeman how you met Jessie, dear," said Mrs Madden encouragingly.

"I met her on the cliffs the first day she came, then she came back the next day and I took her to school. I knew she'd come one day."

"How did you know?"

"I just did."

"Or perhaps you dreamt it?"

Lisa smiled wistfully. "Sometimes it was like a dream," she said. The policeman gave a satisfied grunt. "I see. And you ran away with her to The Sands, is that right?"

"Yes. Jessie lived there."

"How did you get there?"

"I can't tell you. No one must go there, Danny wants to be left alone."

"You have to tell me. It's important. If you really went there. If you really know."

"Careful, constable," said Mrs Madden warningly.

"I do know but I can't tell you."

"I see," said the policeman with another satisfied grunt. "You told your father that this alleged girl had 'gone forever'. What did you mean?"

"She won't come back. Her mother came for her."

"Mother? So there were three of them out there?"

"No. Just Jessie and her father. Jessie's mother went away when she was a baby." The policeman glanced at Mrs Madden. It all seemed to be fitting into place. Morgan had told him about Lisa's mother, told him how Lisa used to invent imaginary friends. She had obviously invented a whole family exactly like her own out on The Sands. There was just one other thing he had to clear up.

"Where did Jessie go?"

"She went back to the sea."

"You mean she drowned!"

"No! She wanted to go when the time came!"

"If she went in the sea she must have drowned. Who made her go? *Who drowned Jessie?*"

Lisa gave a little scream, Mrs Madden went to her. "That's enough," she said to the policeman. "Please leave at once."

"Let her answer that question first."

"Jessie couldn't drown," said Lisa, getting worked up. "She wasn't like other people. Why do you ask horrible questions about her, you don't believe in her...Danny couldn't even bear to watch her go. Leave him alone!"

"Now see what you've done," said Mrs Madden, pushing the policeman out through the door. "Just when she was getting so much better!"

She went back to comfort Lisa. "Never mind, Lisa. Don't upset yourself, lie down now, I'll get you some medicine."

"He said terrible things...said Danny...Danny

drowned Jessie...or I did! Jessie was my friend! Danny didn't want her to go..."

"Did you see her go, Lisa?" Mrs Madden asked gently.

"No. She didn't want us to. She went when the storm started, suddenly. She knew her mother had come. She felt it earlier, when the bells rang under the sea and her seagull flew away."

"Seagulls do fly away, dear."

"Not like this. He flew away suddenly and forever, Jessie knew that. Please make them leave Danny alone, ma'am, please!"

Mrs Madden smiled. "Don't talk about it any more, Lisa. It's all over, isn't it? Try not to think about it. Pretend it was all a dream and soon everyone will forget anything ever happened. Wouldn't it be best that way?"

"Yes," said Lisa thankfully. She didn't want to be asked any more questions. She wanted to keep Jessie and Danny to herself...and Max.

Harry came to see her one afternoon, bringing a book and an apple. Mrs Madden was pleased. She had tried to get some of the girls to visit Lisa but they had backed away frightened and made up flimsy excuses. Not Harry, he had asked to see her. Mrs Madden watched him go cautiously up the staircase, thinking there goes another loner, like Lisa. They had much in common, perhaps they could be friends.

Harry hovered uneasily in Lisa's room. "It's big," he said, "ever so big for one person. Here...I brought you these." He thrust the book and the apple towards her and backed away again quickly.

"Thank you, that's kind. Are you staying...I mean ...why aren't you at school?"

"School's shut. Miss Potter's gone and we're going to have a new teacher!"

"Good! I'm glad!"

"So'm I!" They started to laugh and then Lisa glanced at the door. "Shhh! Mrs Madden might hear. Why's she going?"

Harry relaxed and pulled a stool close to Lisa's bed. "She had this funny turn after you went away with ...her...with Jessie. Her eyes went big and her face crumpled like this..." He made such a grotesque face that Lisa had to stuff the sheet in her mouth to stop herself laughing out loud.

"And then?"

"Then the doctor came and took her away. Next day the parson came and we had prayers and such and then he sort of preached about evil...and raising spirits and how God didn't like it."

"Why did he do that?"

"He was saying...about Jessie...that we'd heard things in the village and just imagined she was there! So I said...but Miss Potter *spoke* to her, and he got angry and said I was impertinent and anyway Miss Potter had been ill. But Lisa, the others all agreed. They said she hadn't really been there."

Lisa shrugged and turned away. Harry was puzzled. "You went to The Sands, you did, didn't you? What was it like?"

"I'm not sure now, Harry. I've been ill, I can't remember, maybe I dreamt it all."

"No! Lisa, you used to tell me about The Sands, you *brought* Jessie, why have you changed? Did you hear the bells? Are you frightened?"

"Sorry, Harry, I can't tell you, I can't be sure..."

"Well, *I* saw Jessie," Harry said, angry with disappointment. "My Grandma Rose spoke to her, she knew where she came from."

"Blind Rose...she used to live on The Sands..."

"She doesn't like anyone to know that. She doesn't remember it anyway...so she says."

"Max!" said Lisa suddenly. "Harry, will you do something for me? Ask Max to come, I can't ask Mrs Madden. Bring him when...what's wrong?" Harry was edging towards the door.

"Nothing...I have to go, I'm late..."

"No, wait. There's something...Harry! What's happened to Max?"

"Don't ask me. I wasn't to tell you," Harry said, fiddling with the door latch and wishing he had never come.

"You haven't told me," Lisa said quietly. "When did he die?"

"Last week."

"Last week when?"

"When you went...when you weren't here. He was in the Infirmary, he was ever so old and sick, Lisa."

"Yes," she said, staring at nothing, but with a look in her eyes that frightened Harry. "He came to bring me back. Dead Man's Walk... It was Max. It was him."

Harry scuttled out of the parsonage like a terrified dormouse. Lisa was odd, she was frighteningly odd. He didn't want to know about The Sands any more, he didn't want to be haunted like Lisa.

Lisa was sad about Max. He had led her to Jessie in the first place, and in the end he had led her away from The Sands. Now Max had gone and the link was broken. There was no one—not even Harry—who wanted to believe that Jessie had ever existed. Lisa smiled a little to herself. It had all been a dream. She would never speak of Jessie again and Danny would be left in peace on The Sands.

Jessie was her secret alone now. Lisa took the folded sheet of paper from its hiding place in the hollow bed post, and spread it out. The ink had run when it got wet, but Jessie's neat writing was still clear. It was Lisa's good fortune that no one had found it in her clothes, good fortune that no one at school remembered Jessie writing, or saw Lisa take the sheet of paper at school. What had Jessie said to Miss Potter?

"Danny says I shouldn't copy. I should always make things out of my own head. I'll write about the dream I had last night."

# My Dream

by Jessie Bates

I dreamed about the sea again last night. Not the friendly waves, but the very deepest depths where it is dark and there is mystery and something that calls out to you if you choose to listen.

In my dream the sea was calling me to go back to Dead Man's Walk. The sea was high and I was afraid to go. But I had heard it call and so I had to go. The waves were thrashing, black and angry, against the rocks below. Each one reached higher than the last, reached up to grab me in its great curled finger tips. I screamed and tried to cling to the rock face because I thought the Sea Monster was lying waiting below and he was laughing, laughing at me for I was hanging in his space.

Sometimes in dreams you fall very fast, or you can fly away. But this dream stopped for a little while. I felt my mother close and I wanted to be with her. The wave had come for me. I wanted to go but I wanted to go back to Danny, and I woke up screaming because they were pulling me different ways. Pulling, pulling so hard that I woke up screaming for my mother and Danny was standing in my doorway.

"Why are you calling out to your mother?" he asked.

"It was just a dream," I told him, "just a bad dream." But I knew the dream would come again and I might have to leave him. Danny went on looking at me from my doorway. He would not come to comfort me as he had always done before.

"Don't cry, Jessie," he said. "It was not a dream. You will be happy and I know how to be alone.

"Please stop crying now, you cannot change what has to happen. It is not your fault.

"You are a child of the sea."